Out of Line

Imaginative Writings

ON

PEACE AND JUSTICE

EDITED BY
SAM LONGMIRE

GARDEN HOUSE PRESS

www.gardenhousepress.com

Out of Line

ACKNOWLEDGEMENTS

Cover art, "Ancestral Spirit Dance," is by Willis "Bing" Davis. He lives in Dayton, Ohio, where he grew up. After teaching in the Dayton Public Schools and at DePauw and Miami Universities, Davis joined the faculty at Central State University where he served as Chair of the Art Department and Director of the Paul Robeson Cultural and Performing Arts Center. He is currently President of the Board of Directors of the National Conference of Artists.

Davis' achievements as an artist and curator are impressive. Through ceramics, drawing, painting, photography, and jewelry, his art is a mosaic of black culture, both African and American. His work is included in collections in the United States, Canada, Japan, Germany, France, Senegal, Ghana, Nigeria, and Gabon, Africa. He has had exhibitions in numerous galleries including Studio Museum of Harlem, Renwick Gallery, American Craft Museum, Maryland Institute College of Art, and National Museum of Art of Senegal West Africa. Davis curated the groundbreaking exhibition *Uncommon Beauty in Common Objects: The Legacy of African-American Craft Art* that toured the United States. He has received numerous awards including the Honorary Doctorate of Fine Arts from Maryland Institute College of Fine Arts, Adrian College, DePauw University, and University of Dayton.

The photograph by Muriel Blaisdell on the back cover shows the National AFSC touring exhibition *Eyes Wide Open*. On display from Sept.23-28 in Dayton, Ohio, at the Cross Creek Community Church, this powerful exhibit is still attracting attention all over the country because of its very simple and powerful message on war in general, and the Iraq war in particular. The visual images of the combat boots and representation of Iraqi shoes is a compelling reminder of the cost of war in lives.

Barbara Roberts
American Friends Service Committee
Dayton, Ohio

Out of Line

Table of Contents

TABLE OF CONTENTS

Part I Private Worlds

Every Story Is Mine *Cervine* 7

When Powers Clash *Bolstridge* 8

Clean *Hoffman* 16

Peacekeeper *Wilson* 17

The Boxer *Morrill* 25

Outside Block *Campbell* 26

Tiny and Hard and Never Angry *Guidry* 27

Hospice Nursing 102 *Subraman* 37

Bedelia *Moffett* 38

Part II What In the World Are We Doing?

September 11, 2001 *Subraman* 50

Detasseling Crew *Morris* 52

White Rice *Shook* 53

Wounded Knee *Monson* 54

To A Case Worker *Littlecrow-Russell* 55

Imitation Eagle Feathers *Littlecrow-Russell* 56

Midwestern Conversations *Worra* 57

Fells Point *Gavin* 58

Downsized *Barrett* 63

Chocolate *Barrett* 64

Drifters *Barrett* 65
Just the Boys *Dacey* 67
A Day on the Mall *Trout* 68
This Is What Democracy Looks Like *Franklin* 77
On Strike *McBride* 79
The Monetary News *Whalen* 80
Edward Teller, Father of Nearly Nothing *Bradley* 81

Part III   A World Gone Mad

A Child Must Be Taught *Larson* 83
The Coat *Zimet* 84
Yarn for Bosnia *Zimet* 86
General Store in Wartime *Flannery* 87
Knowing The Bomb So Well *Monaghan* 88
Geography Lessons *Monaghan* 89
Quilting Towards Armageddon *Berkey-Abbott* 91
Forgetting *Radavich* 92
Peace is so much harder than war *D'Alessio* 93
Prayer as Tanks Slouch Toward Baghdad
   Sornberger 94
RAGING GRANNIES *Powers* 96
THE FIELD ARTILLERYMAN *Powers* 97
War in the Garden *Bjorlie* 98
The Land Between the Rivers *Bjorlie* 99
THE BUILD-UP *Fisher* 100

Repentance *Christianson* 101

The Poet During War   *Ross* 102

Quicksand   *Kincaid* 103

THE OTHER SIDE *Gastiger* 104

WORDS FOR THE ABANDONED   *Gastiger* 105

Thirteen ways of looking at Baghdad   *Lause* 106

Once upon a field   *Levine* 109

Buchanan at the monkey house   *Casey* 110

Part IV   A World View

Mr. Yamamoto's Painting   *Rothschild* 111

Little Hannalore   *Garavente* 112

All Will Abide   *Madigan* 121

Grief *Peckham* 125

Ibrahim's Story   *Newman* 128

FROM THE FIRST WEEKS IN NEW YORK, IF MY GRANDFATHER COULD HAVE WRITTEN A POSTCARD   *Lifshin* 128

The Barn   *Onart* 130

The Police Station   *Onart* 131

Lenin Hospital   *Onart* 132

The Lesson   *Sorescu* 134

 (Translated by Sorkin and Vianu)

Always Bearded   *Sorescu* 135

 (Translated by Sorkin and Vianu)

The Meet   *Sorescu* 136
   (Translated by Sorkin and Vianu)
Nose Print   *Sorescu* 137
   (Translated by Sorkin and Ştefănescu)
The Exile Season   *Anhalt* 141

Part V   Natural and Human Worlds

On Earth Day 2003   *Seltzer* 146
Uses for Gypsum   *Carter* 147
Snow Drops   *Reid* 148
Spring Trumps World News, May 2003   *Flannery* ... 149
Morning Briefings   *Husted* 150
Lessons   *Milosevic* 151
Annual Pigeon Shoot, Higgins, PA   *Shapiro* 152
Radio News   *Lang* 153
Full Circle   *Case* 154
Prairie Storms   *Zydek* 155
Visiting the Niagara   *Zydek* 156

Part VI   Creating A Better World

Post 9/11: Trauma, Nonviolence and
   Self-Protection   *Morr-Wineman* 157
Shit Work   *Littlecrow-Russell* 168
Alabama Bound   *Rozga* 169
Eulogy for Prathia Hall Wynn   *Morris* 170
Peace March   *Cervine* 171

Aging *Subraman* 172

NO MORE AIDS *Pattengale* 173

Our Lady of Sorrows *Flannery* 174

What to Say About Jake *Buttenwieser* 177

Praise *Press* 185

Eve *Press* 186

The House in Roskilde *Pucciani* 187

A Learned Response *Ballard* 189

The Garden *Ballard* 190

Contributors 191

Out of Line

PRIVATE WORLDS

I

Every Story Is Mine

Dane Cervine

Fearless, I open the newspaper another day,
unroll the modern parchment, this divine scroll,
unfathomable. A quick scan of the headlines,
the fine print of each obituary.

There is never enough tragedy
to ensure your own safety.

Dressing for work, I pray the day's gauntlet
escapes the evening news, that I return home
unscathed, intact.

Fate is impenetrable. This is why every horoscope,
tea leaf, chicken bone clattering to the ground as dice
holds such fascination—will we become
what we fear, what we hope?

Every step away brings me closer to what I run from.

If I were to let the world roll through me as a flood,
would I be saved, or merely drown?

There are no answers to such questions,
though the front page begs each one.

I finger each tattered edge, laughing, crying.
Every story is mine.

When Powers Clash

Alice Bolstridge

When the planes crashed into the World Trade Building and the Pentagon and rural Pennsylvania, I was writing and worrying about the quality of care my son Moonway receives. I worry that, in spite of acclaimed advances in the biological treatment of the mentally ill, medication primarily sedates Moonway's behavior; it does not relieve the symptoms he suffers. I worry about declining health from side effects of medication, and from hygiene and dietary habits that grow out of delusions, fears, fatigue, and depression. I worry about social, emotional, and spiritual health. And, as much as I worry about all of this, I worry about the quality of the relationship he has with his care providers, a relationship that often requires aggressive peace-making among the various factions responsible for his care. I worry that his treatment team meetings, some of the treatment decisions, and some of the attitudes expressed, all aggravate, rather that treat, his other problems.

His current treatment is complicated by the prospect that he may (others say <u>will</u>) remain a ward of the Federal Court for the rest of his life, a probation officer will be a permanent part of his treatment team, and treatment can be legally forced at any time. When I emerged from my writing session and realized what happened in New York, Washington, and Pennsylvania, I remembered Moonway's respect and admiration for skyjackers; I remembered that, depending on how he is feeling on any particular day, Moonway tells different stories about the charge that got him involved with the federal court system. Times he is feeling persecuted, he says, "I never threatened anyone. I was framed by the police because I was waving a toy gun and a knife in front of Burger King." But talking to me about this essay, he admitted, "I was in jail for calling in bomb threats, and I wrote to the senator's staff and threatened to have their reproductive organs twisted off with a pair of pliers if they didn't get me out. It was all crazy. Nuts."

So I decided to check on how he was doing with the news of the suicide attacks. When I got to his apartment, he said he was on his way to go make copies of some things. I asked how he was doing with the news of the plane-crash bombings. He said angrily, "I'm OK, Mom. I got to go." He knew I was checking on him, and he resented it.

I went on with the chores and errands I had scheduled for the day. I did laundry and some banking, shopped for groceries. A TV or radio played the hi-jacking news everywhere I went. At home, I folded clothes in front of the TV and wept at images of people so hopeless they jumped out of top-floor windows. I wept at the despair and grief on faces of people searching for loved ones. I wept that we can think of nothing better, more effective, than deadly force to respond to the most deadly of our relationship problems. Is it odd to speak of a catastrophic terrorist attack as our relationship problem?

And I wept that Moonway's relationship with his treatment team can so easily go awry as it did over the course of the nine months leading up to a court appearance. When confronted with his increasing isolation, deteriorating hygiene, intensified belief system at odds with social reality, and refusal to participate in group therapy and cooperate with the treatment plan, the probation officer along with some of Moonway's care providers could think of nothing more effective than force to solve the problems, and they filed a petition with the Federal Court to require him to comply or risk full guardianship or incarceration again.

Fortunately, spring came and with it, as it does with most of us, a renewed energy for Moonway. He was soon socializing more, disturbing his neighbors less, and taking better care of himself and his apartment. By the time of the court date in July, his behavior was more compliant than in the dark days of winter. The judge had obviously read Moonway's complete file and was a person capable of taking a long view. He could see how Moonway has improved in these recent years in his behavior toward public officials; he suggested that the petition be withdrawn, which it was. He praised Moonway for his improvement and encouraged him to keep up the good work. His treatment team was subsequently reconstituted with much more friendly attitudes. This episode looks like it had a happy ending.

It did. But the longer course of his relationship with care providers continues to be problematic. And his situation is not unique. There are many unresolved problems in the treatment of people with chronic mental illness. All medicine is essentially experimental, a matter of using trial and error to search out the best combination of drugs to control the most troublesome symptoms; there is nothing like one best medicine for any particular set of symptoms. And all psychiatric medicine is very risky in terms of side effects. Staff at Mental Health Centers across the country are under trained, overworked, and underpaid. From all I can see, our own Center in this area is much better than most. Moonway is lucky to see a psychiatrist once a month for fifteen minutes and sometimes in a crisis more often. Except in the earliest days of his illness, before he was adjudged "chronic," he has rarely seen a psychotherapist. Yet, all studies show a combination of therapy and medication is the most effective treatment we now know. Many patients like Moonway see even less than he does of the most highly qualified professionals. People with chronic mental illnesses are relegated to custodial-care workers who struggle to solve such living problems as Moonway was experiencing acutely last winter. They see their role as primarily living-skills trainers and are not competent to provide psychotherapeutic care or deal with motivation problems. When their training does not solve the problems, they see few alternatives and give patients few choices. From attendance at meetings of Moonway's treatment team and of The National Alliance of the Mentally Ill, I know the relationship among health care providers, patients, and their families too often feels adversarial on all sides. Patients and their families too often feel intimidated, burdened, and coerced by the mental health systems that are trying to help them.

I witnessed a session between Moonway and one of these providers that offers an example of this. She said,"Moonway, you didn't have enough food stamps last month to last all month. What are you doing to budget them now?"

He said, "I'm saving some up for later in the month."
She said, "But what are you doing to budget them?"
He said, "Saving them up."
She said, "But that isn't budgeting. What are you doing to budget them?"
This went on for several interminable moments until he quit trying entirely to respond to her. She then tried to ask him about cleaning his apartment. He said, "I need to go smoke."
While he was gone, she turned to me and said, "What did you think of his apartment last time you were in?"
I said, "It was cleaner than last winter."
She said, "How about the kitchen?"
I said, "I didn't go in the kitchen."
She said, "The garbage was overflowing when I was there. And the bathroom?"
I said, "He had even swept the stairs." I felt interrogated, and I wanted to go smoke, though I quit smoking years ago.
And there was another session with this worker when Moonway asked about the court hearing, "Why can't we shift this shit against the government doing this to me, so we'll all be in agreement?"
She said, "This is going to go on forever, Moonway. A lifetime. No end date on it. We're going to be doing this over and over and over again. But like I told you, don't worry about it. It's like a formality we have to go through. And it's all for your own good."
I want to give this worker the benefit of the doubt and think she was trying to encourage him to live in reality. But I can't get past the fact of her totally ignoring Moonway's distress, the feelings of hopelessness and discouragement, behind his question. At that moment, her response to him could only have intensified his need to retreat from reality. Still, I was gratified to hear him say "Thank you" for her offer to help with the appointments. She didn't, however, carry through with those offers. Moonway made his own appointment with the eye doctor, and I made one for a physical. Many times providers do not follow through.
I believe this worker and her methods typify the quality of

custodial care. She worried a lot about Moonway. She wanted him to do well. She expressed a good deal of anxiety and frustration when he didn't. But she focused on problems and failures and how to fix them. I only rarely heard her comment on his strengths or successes, and then only after I asked her to do so. She did not know how to accomplish her goals for him, and she didn't know how to respond to his emotional and psychological needs. Residential-care staff and community support counselors are the lowest paid professionals in the mental health system. They spend the most time with patients. The quality of their relationship to patients is the most important.

 Moonway's probation officer knows very little about psychiatric illnesses, and, coming from a law enforcement model, he plays the tough authoritarian role on the team. His presence on the treatment team was a constant threat that Moonway could be sent back to the Medical Center for Federal Prisoners, and the relationship between them was constantly tense.

 Moonway's psychiatrist has more respect and compassion for Moonway, but she is one of the highest paid professionals, which makes her time too valuable to the agency to waste it nurturing a relationship with clients who have chronic and serious illnesses.

 Moonway retreats from treatment team meetings often to go smoke. He feels "interrogated" by them, and he has come to see "psyche and corrections" as torturers. I, myself, often feel the tension and stress of meetings is so high that I wish I could escape. Under the influence of Xavier Amador's book, *I'm Not Sick, I Don't Need Help*, I have suggested at team meetings that we all work on improving our relationship with him. Show respect for his emotional and artistic needs to express himself and to be heard and understood. Consider ways the team could link recommended treatment to what Moonway feels his needs are. Consider offering treatment options, rather than just requirements. Offer more hope and encouragement. Apply peace-making strategies.

 I was too subtle in my efforts, too peaceful. Focusing on Moonway's noncompliance, the principal antagonists on the team seemed deaf to all my requests. I felt ignored except once when his financial conservator and I were praising his improvements, and his psycho-neurological evaluator said, "Oh, I suppose he is all better now, and we have no more work to do here. We can all go home." Such sarcasm is intended to silence, and it did. The focus on strengths stopped, and the team returned to a discussion of non-compliance and how to force compliance. I believe tough love can be effective treatment. It's necessary to be firm (tough) about setting clear limits with Moonway and maintaining them. But tough without love feels like persecution, even to me.

Fortunately, Moonway has a long-time relationship with an advocate, another treatment-team member, who was away attending to the death of parents during the most troublesome times that spring. With the team, he doesn't try to be as subtle as I do, and when he did return, he took up the cause of treating Moonway better, as he has before many times. It was primarily his in-your-face efforts that got the happy ending in court. And, at his urging, a neglected 1998 report from an occupational therapist surfaced and supported all of my requests about Moonway's care. In her report there is an explanation for many of the persisting symptoms and recommendations for how care providers can work with him. He is at the moment being treated with a good deal more respect by his care providers. Maybe there is reason to hope, but my peaceful efforts went unheard. It took aggressive advocacy to succeed.

I am mostly a peaceful person. I believe in respectfully negotiating no-lose solutions in which all participants are heard and respected. But, feeling unheard and not respected, when I remember that sarcastic comment that silenced talk of Moonway's strengths, I imagine myself slamming the book in the speaker's face with such force I hear bone crack. I feel paranoid. I want to attack. I want to hurt. I don't often allow such imaginings into consciousness. But they come readily when I summon them in order to understand the mentality of the ignored and disrespected. If I were diagnosed with chronic schizophrenia, I would not dare admit this. But I am a senior citizen with a long and respected record as a teacher and other evidence of high functioning, and I hope I can get away with it. I hope my freedom-of-speech rights are safe. I hope no one is likely to fear me as someone who acts out these imaginings. The opinions, thoughts, and feelings of the chronically mentally ill are routinely ignored, dismissed, or taken as evidence of paranoia and considered dangerous. So are those of international antagonists, on both sides.

Social and political insanity in our institutions produces the most troubling issues of our time world wide: horrifying experiences in wars, environmental crises, starvation-level poverty, routine oppression of the least powerful by the more powerful. These kinds of cultural issues provide the sources of Moonway's symbolic system and fascinations with Hitler, skyjackers, Manson, and various other terrorists. I think it no coincidence that Moonway wants to target Hollywood with a 9-11 type attack—Hollywood, the maker of popular myth, the manufacturer of our cultural consciousness. Moonway wants to do unto them as he feels he has been done to by "psyche and corrections" and by all the madness he witnesses in the world via the media. Indeed, the personal is social and political and vice versa, and no single instance of mental illness is just a personal matter.

Suicide sky jackers may or may not be mentally ill. I won't try, here, to argue that all evil or wrong doing is a symptom of mental illness, though it may be. Nor that we should try to negotiate with terrorists, though maybe we should, but by the time the planes crash or the bombs go off, it is too late for negotiations. My point is that nations in international crisis, all sides in the crisis, exhibit paranoid fears, power cravings, and power mongering behaviors: feelings of being disrespected, victimized, and persecuted motivate cycles of attack and counter attack—war.

When whole subcultures of people will support and help to coordinate attacks like this against us, we clearly have relationship problems. Haven't we known this for a long time? I mourn that it has come to this crisis, again. I mourn that the only thing they can think of to get attention in the face of perceived injustice against them is to attack with force. I mourn that the only thing we can think of is to retaliate with force. I mourn our human inability to dissolve the hatred between us.

I wonder what the world would look like if we were willing to focus a fraction of the attention and resources that we devote to fighting our enemies to discovering solutions to relationship problems—the personal, the social, the institutional, the political. I pray that we find a will somewhere to try it for the sake of all the world's mental health.

Clean

Barbara Hoffman

at 96th and 1st
the Triboro Bridge arches
away from the city
my red Datsun blows smoke
into the cold December night
windows closed tight

a man with a squeegee
shuffles between the lines of cars
dreared eyes   unshaven boy-man face
strips of scarves wrapped
in a ragged turban around his head

he peers in
breathing on my car window
breathing on my way of life
I look away

never lock eyes

he waves the squeegee
in the air
his face a question
my head shakes no

never speak

a penny   he mumbles
a penny

Peacekeeper

Judy Wilson

    Here it is then—the evidence my husband's been waiting for—the major screw-up I cannot excuse—the one I cannot defend my son against. Hard physical proof for him to say, *You see? You finally see how it is? I'm right—I've been right all along.* Yet it is not my son—his stepson—that I despise stepping through the stench of dog piles and Mud Slide bottles and broken glass from the ceiling fixtures, but my husband I could choke, could squeeze his muscled neck to stop the mouth in that well-trimmed beard, not another word. We'd just driven nine hundred miles back from visiting his parents through all of Christmas and New Year's, had lugged the twins, Jamie and James, in from the car, tucked them in bed, and I'm looking at the house, the damage really for the first time.
    "That goddamned little shit," Daniel says and kicks the wall, the cheap print in its cheap frame slipping to the floor.
    "Daniel—"
    "No, uh-uh, no Daniel—this is our *home*. Goddammit. He's fucked up good this time. Might as well have walked up and slapped me in the face."
    He's holding Zim, a kestrel hawk, my hawk, my now dead hawk, scooped from the bottom of its tall cage, and my husband stands there stroking the blue wings, the rusty cap of its head. I cup my hands and wince as he puts Zim in my open palms. The bird is warm against my fingers. I can hardly believe it's dead. I press its breast with my thumb—still soft—pluck its talons with my pinky—still pliable. Not long dead. Daniel stands beside me, his hands in his pockets, rattling keys and change. He's biting the inside of his cheek, his eyes puddling, looking from the bird to the wrecked house then back to me, his lips pressed firm to keep them from trembling, his heart breaking for me or the bird or our house—I can't tell which. It could be the cumulative effect of it. It might be that. I hand Zim back to him and step past, picking up a fast food bag lying empty on the floor, the thirteenth bag so far. A large gathering.

"Baby, I know you loved this bird," he says, taking Zim back from me, rubbing Zim's breast with his thumb, ruffling then smoothing the small speckled feathers there.

He knows nothing. It was just a bird. To hell with the bird. Where is my son? I ball up the paper bag in my hand—a nice, tight round—then drop it back on the floor. Fifteen hours, straight through the night, and daylight is beginning to show through the windows. I don't have it in me to do this now.

"He probably didn't feed it. Just didn't feed it—that's all. Didn't feed the dogs. You see the dog food bag? Poor dogs had to tear into the bag to get to their food," he says.

The lab and the beagle are panting with joy to see us. The dogs could fast for a week and still be overweight. There are dog piles everywhere; they certainly digested something.

He lays Zim gingerly in the bottom of his cage and wraps big arms around me, rocking me in little jerks. I get my hands up and pat his back lightly. It's the best I can do now, facing this, knowing what comes next. I cannot blame him. Not now—not after this.

"I'll start cleaning this up," he says. "You go shower—climb into bed." Then he goes to the window and, with a grunt, slides it open. "Cold as it is, we gotta open everything up," he says and heads down the hallway, for another window, everything under control.

The cold settles in. I stand and stare at Zim in the bottom of the cage.

"Couldn't even let the dogs out," he says, coming back down the hallway. "Probably been out partying since we've been gone. Well, he's fucked me over for the last time. That's it. I hope you know, that's it."

I'd pulled the note down before he'd had a chance to see it: *Mom, gone to coast. New Year's party. Back soon. Love you, Wes.* It's January third. And gone, as if nothing had gone wrong here. As if the door frame wasn't broken between the kitchen and dining room, as if the cords hadn't been cut from the lamps in the living room, as if there weren't cigarette burns in the new linen tablecloth and my comforter, and the rug in the den, as if beer hadn't been spilled all over the computer keyboard and printer, as if—everywhere I look there is more. He won't come home. Not to live. He'll know this—that he must not come home to live. He'll call me. He'll come see me. But he's made his mighty move.

I slap my thigh and the beagle follows me. I start pulling off my sweatshirt, heading for the shower. Towels are scattered and I study the bathtub, not knowing who or what was in it last. I pull my sweatshirt back over my head, pat my leg again, and the beagle follows me to the bedroom. I close the drapes, their dark green thickness blocking the morning light and rest on the side of my bed. Like a ragdoll, I bend to take off my shoes, then stretch out under the warmth of the covers. My husband, in some other room, curses in sharp whispers now and then. I pull a pillow over my head—nothing to give, nothing to say. Sleep is what I need. But it isn't likely to come—not completely. There will be a restlessness in my mind now that may never go away. Does it ever go away? There are pills in the cabinet. I could sleep. Soundly. But I must be ready. For what, I don't know, for anything, for everything now. The possibilities overwhelm me. With the windows open, I hear the train running the track five miles to the east. The beagle jumps onto the bed, curls into the bend of my legs, and I reach down to take his ear in my hand. He doesn't like it, but I indulge myself.

In the next room, my husband's on the cordless phone with his mother, the floor giving, squeaking, as he paces: *She's shattered. The bird dead and all. He's done it this time. I've bent over backwards for that boy, you know I have. Nobody can say I haven't tried. I can only take so much. And that's it. This is it. Let that little shit walk back into this house. No, uh-uh, it's on now.*

Pat yourself on the back, dear, Mr. Perfect. Poor Mr. Perfect, saddled all these years with a bad kid, a bad seed, a kid the Pope himself would have cast off years ago.

Pope: Wes, are you aware that a hundred dollars is missing from my coin pouch?

Wes: A hundred? You keep a hundred dollars in your coin pouch? Man, Pope, that's not a real smart thing to do, you know?

Pope: Perhaps not. Nice running shoes, Wes. They must have

cost at least a hundred dollars, am I right?

Wes: Oh, man, at least! But Josh's mom spoils him; kid gets everything. He must have five or six pairs like this. He let me borrow these.

Then, two weeks later:

Pope: Wes, I see you still haven't returned Josh's shoes to him.

Wes: No, see, look at this little black mark here on the side. See that. Got some grease or something on 'em. Not that bad, I didn't think. But Josh told me keep 'em. Said he didn't want 'em back messed up like that. He's picky, I swear.

Money missing, ten here, twenty there—if that were all. But I've seen Wes in County Jail orange coveralls; I've gone down alleys and up outdoor staircases, seeking out a bail bonds-woman in a smoke-filled, comic strip hole-in-the-wall office; I've pulled in favors from friends to get in the door of the best lawyer in town, maxing out credit cards to come up with his retainment fee. And if nine thousand dollars wasn't what I'd have to come up with if he didn't show in court in two weeks, maybe I could sleep now. But I doubt it.

The light comes on in the room, and Daniel, unaware of Wes's original sins, except for the missing money here and there, says, "You awake? Mom wants to say hello to you." He walks across the room, handing the phone to me.

We just left there yesterday—what could there be to talk about––maybe we left something behind, a pair of the twin's socks, the umbrella. No, I clearly remember packing the umbrella.

I prop up on my elbow. "Hullo, mom." The beagle is struggling to get out from under the weight of my leg.

"I just wanted to tell you how sorry I am about everything. Are you all right?"

"Yeah—need some sleep—but I'm okay."

"Well, I know how much you loved Zim. I'm sorry about your bird. And Daniel said your house is pretty torn up?"

There's more than one way to fuck-up a house—this one was fucked long ago. I care fuck-all for the bird or the house right now.

"Yeah, bird's gone. And, yeah, house is a mess. But we'll get it cleaned up. Nothing that can't be fixed or replaced," I say.

"Well, you know kids will do that to you—seems like they're always breaking their mother's hearts."

"It'll be all right, I'm sure. Thanks for caring, though. Here's Daniel."

I jerk the phone to Daniel and fall back on my pillow. I cover my ear with another and say, "Could you shut the door on your way out?"

Ten minutes later, Daniel is back in my face. "Shouldn't you call your folks? Let them know we got home okay?"

"I gave them the signal, Daniel, the two rings, hang-up, two rings, remember?"

"But don't you think it would make you feel better if you talked to them? You know? Let them know what's going on?"

I sit straight up in the bed, slapping down at the puffy comforter. "No—it would not make me feel better. It would make me feel lousy, goddamned lousy, and I'm sure your mother will call right over there. What *will* make me feel better is sleep. Please." The beagle stretches and rearranges himself on the bed and I think—see, even the dog can't sleep.

One of the twins, it's Jamie, comes tumbling onto the bed. "Why's it all so messy?" she asks.

I fall back, put the pillow over my face.

Daniel pats my leg, "I got the kids. Sleep."

Suddenly, the pillow is pulled from my face, a wet kiss meets my forehead, and the pillow falls back into place again. I hear the door close quietly and Daniel whispering to the twins on the other side of it. I move the pillow to my chest and hug it, looking up at the dim ceiling. I am so tired of good intentions.

I cannot sleep. I am lying here, weepy with exhaustion, but I cannot do it. My head throbs with wonder and worry—where is he? Is he in trouble? in jail? hurt? depressed? I stomp to the bathroom. This will be me now, forever dickering through the medicine cabinet. Get the little pill, that tough, tiny pill. I feel warmth from the mirror lights as I tilt my head back, working the pill to the back of my throat. I reach for a cup from the dispenser, but the dispenser is empty. The pill is dissolving into a bitter paste on the back of my tongue, and I turn on the faucet, leaning over the sink, frantically scooping water into my mouth, then remember that I hadn't washed my hands since I'd held dead Zim. *Jesus*, I think.

Jamie throws open the bedroom door as I'm drying my face. "Mommy's up!"

"No darling. Mommy is down. Down, down, down. In fact, Mommy may not be . . . never mind. I got up for some water. I need sleep, sweetie. It was a long drive, drove all the way by myself. Can you imagine that?" I bend and hug her to my knees. "You need to brush your hair. Go. Brush your hair."

She follows me back to the bed. "Why didn't Daddy drive some?"

"I didn't want Daddy to drive because Daddy has a bad temper when he drives and he gets nutso. Now you go ask him what nutso means and all that. And brush your hair. Please."

"Where's Wes?"

I pretend to straighten the covers. What to say? Go ask your wonderful father?

"Don't know really. Let Mommy rest now, huh?"

Sleep comes, but it's all still there, billowing in my head, the years of Wes's growing-pain screw-ups, more than a decade's worth of anger in the making: Wes breaking his hand on the brick of the house to keep from hitting his stepfather; Daniel daring over and over; me trying to put two pieces of different puzzles together. I cannot pretend any longer that peace will come between them, that they will fall into place one day. It's been a broken mess from the beginning.

A son's warm kiss on my cheek—something sweet in my dreaming, but no, he has come to me, kneeling beside the bed, his face unshaven, rough. He lays his head on my stomach. He cannot look at me. I put my arm around his thin shoulders and prop up in the bed.

"Where's Daniel? The twins?" I whisper.

He rises and sits on the side of the bed. "Gone. I've been waiting for him to leave. Probably took the twins out to eat. It's about lunch time."

"Are you all right? Jesus Christ, what the hell happened?"
"I don't know."
"What do you mean you don't know? You weren't here?"
"I was here."
"Then what happened?"

"New Year's Eve. I asked a couple friends over to shoot fireworks. But everybody started coming. I didn't know most of them. I kept saying, `You guys gotta go,' but I passed out on the living room floor."

Christ, I think, no explanation is going to be enough—this is bullshit—and there is more to explain—the bird, the dogs, the party on the coast—how could he just leave the house like this? Without any attempt to clean up? We sit, both of us staring at our hands.

"I'm staying with a guy named Bain right now. He got me a job working with him," he says. "Tying steel. I can't come back here. Him and me, Jesus, one of us will end up dead."

"What about college?"

"I'm gonna withdraw. For now." He's picking at his thumbnail.

"No. No, no. You can't do that. If you do that, you'll be proving him right, what he's been saying, *That kid will never finish college.* Wes, you can't do that."

"Just for now. Just till I get you out of here. And the twins. I'm gonna save up and buy the acre next to Bain's place. Get a trailer on it. Then I can get you out of here. You don't need to put up with his shit anymore. And the twins—I'll be damned if he's gonna do to them what he did to me."

I sit up in the bed, dizzy from the pill, and, Christ, for a second, a mere second, I think I see what Daniel sees when he looks at him––the illogic of him, the bumbling puppy-like pawing, scheming him. "Wes—open the curtains, will you?" I turn my feet to the floor, but I can't stand. I sit and watch him, and now I see the him I know well—handsome, full of possibility, full of goodness, really. A good heart. The anger is in him, to be sure, the resentment. How could it not be, after years of Daniel criticizing, humiliating him in public, the drunken fists coming at him, and if not the fists, the feet, and shoves across rooms and out of doors, and dodging tools and cans and whatever else was handy to throw, the lash of belts or branches, the absolute emasculation in front of friends. Years of "you're not gonna make it—you're a worthless little shit." And God knows I'd tried to stop it all, but it was so much bigger than me, the thing that was between them. How can I tell him now that I'm fine here—that Daniel treats me as good as I would expect any husband to treat a wife? Doesn't he see that? No, Christ sake, he thinks I'm trapped, that I've been trapped all these years, that I couldn't get out, didn't have the means to make it on my own with him and then the twins came along. My God, what's he been thinking? Doesn't he see that the man spoils the twins rotten and would never lay a hand on them? Barely ever even raises his voice at them? That he's the only one that Daniel has it in for? It's been my choice to stay, and not only to stay, but to be mostly happy, in spite of how horrible Daniel treated him. I shouldn't have stayed—should never have put a child through it—it would be enough to screw-up any kid, the toughest kid—*but I thought I could fix it.* I should never have married Daniel, and hadn't Wes, little Wes, the Wes before all the mess, cried and pleaded with me not to—had begged me not to get him into this chaos, had seen even then, young as he was, what was to come, and now, what's he saying—*I'll get you out of here*—how did it all get so twisted?

"I hate not to be here for you now," he says. "But I'll do it, Mom. You just hang on." He sits beside me, an arm around me, reaching with his other to rub the lazy beagle. I tilt my head to his shoulder. He seems so grown. When did he grow up? How did he possibly manage to grow up?

The Boxer

Billie Morrill

ROUND ONE
I'm good with my hands,
he said when they met.
Before long,
she was on intimate terms
with his hands,
as they smoothed her hair
from her flushed face,
teased her upturned breasts,
explored her inner thighs.

ROUND TWO
I'm good with my hands,
he convinced the foreman
when he applied
for a job on the line.
For years
he calloused those hands
working double shifts,
while she birthed babies,
one after another.
Tedium washed love
down a river of rye and soda.

ROUND THREE
I'm good with my hands
he bragged to the guys,
bunching those hands into fists
and shadow boxing
in the bar's dark corner.
No one disagreed, picturing

the bruises on his wife's
pretty face . . .
colors that convinced
a sympathetic judge to issue
today's restraining order.

OUTSIDE BLOCK

Douglas G. Campbell

Muscles respond
push my mind aside as
they coordinate their
movements. My right
hand moves towards my
center as fingers simultaneously
curl inward; my hand arcs
upwards protectively
moves across my abdomen,
continues upward blocking
off my chest, throat and chin,
deflecting any incoming threat
directing it to the right, so that I might
counter with an answering
strike. But this movement
is not preemptive, it
does not confront. It is the
answer given when the
demand is not spoken
and when there is no time
to retreat.

Tiny and Hard and Never Angry
Jacqueline Guidry

Her mother's toenails had been so tough, scissors couldn't trim them unless her feet had been soaked and soaked. Now Dalona is amazed to see her own nails yellowing and growing hard against her. She clips after morning showers and wonders how long before even that won't be enough.

After drying, she sits on the toilet seat, foot resting across her thigh as she concentrates on one nail at a time, one after another until a pile of dead clippings mound on the window sill. She thinks about what she can do today after she gets lunch. She touches the pane, warm for the first of November. Her checks will keep her in her apartment, no matter how hard the winter. A blurred picture from that time before the checks and the clinic still creeps into her head when she isn't on guard. Dalona hates those reminders of what her life could be again.

Last year, when April arrived and she finally noticed a pile of clippings on the sill, she decided she had to keep them all year. She liked seeing part of her lining the window through the seasons, not worrying about anything. Was staying in bed all day the right thing or should she go to St. John's or the Perry Center instead? Those nails didn't have to care any more.

Now she brushes the clippings into her cupped hand. The edges of the nails are sharp points. If she decides to sew a fancy church dress, she can use them instead of store bought pins. But then Dalona remembers she doesn't know how to sew any more, not since Mama passed.

Sometimes she doesn't mind thinking of that time—her and Mama walking to the bus stop, the smell of polish on silver, the feel of silk along her fingers as she stole a touch of the lady's blouse or skirt. Most times, though, she likes just thinking about today, not about yesterday. When she'd had her spells, none of Mama's ladies had liked remembering she was there. They wanted Mama, but not Dalona. When Mama passed, they forgot Dalona quicker than they forgot last year's favorite dress.

She dumps her nails in the brown sack next to the stove. The bag is nearly full. One thing she can do today is carry trash to the dumpster back of her building. She'll do it right after lunch because that's when the punks are least likely to be out.

"Crazy old fart," they yell at her when all she's doing is dumping trash. "My old man says your puss stinks," they yell, then laugh, holding their sides as if it's the funniest thing they ever heard. They've never felt silk, even someone else's silk, against their skin. That was the only thing keeping Dalona from chasing their butts out the alley and to their mamas for good whippings.

Back in the bathroom, she pats powder all over herself. She found the unopened box outside Sax's on the Plaza last winter. Some lady, maybe one of Mama's ladies, had dropped it from a bag overflowing with cashmere sweaters and Italian shoes and French perfumes. When she got home, the lady probably hadn't even noticed something was missing. The powder was meant for Dalona. She passes the puff between her toes and over the raw nails, then sprinkles powder in her white gym socks before putting them on. After that, she dresses quickly. Black pants with elastic waist, a smeared mustard stain centered on the belly. Beige checked blouse with a squared off hem and a tie hanging from the collar as had once been the fashion. Finally, tennis shoes.

She's ready, but not sure what to do. Too early for St. John's. She kneels in front of her TV and experiments with different bows. Her reflection on the blank screen makes her feel smaller than usual. If she stares too long at her small self in the set, she might disappear altogether. She's done that before, disappeared from one place and reappeared days, sometimes weeks later in another. One of these days she'll be ready for it to happen again. Just not now, not today, not yet. She ties the strands into a wide, flopping bow and stands quickly before the set can work its magic on her.

Back in the kitchen, she pulls out her apartment key from an empty lima beans can sitting on the counter. She lifts her blouse to tuck the key into her bra. The metal is cold against her skin, but she doesn't mind because it feels real, reassuring. Then she sits on the one chair, flecks of blue paint chips scattered across the back to remind her it had once been a fine thing, and waits. Too early for the bus. She waits in the narrow space of kitchen that holds a squat refrigerator faded to a dull gray from what must have once been white, a stove with only one burner still working, a sink stained brown from the drip that used to keep Dalona awake at night but now soothes her like Mama singing a lullaby, a card table. Dalona knows a real kitchen has a door that leads somewhere besides a bit larger space with a TV and sofa that doubles as a bed and an overhead light covered with a half shade clinging precariously, the other half having cracked off long ago.

It's time now. She reaches for her faded green sweater. Yarn has unraveled around the bottom and two buttons in the middle have fallen off, but Dalona doesn't care. This was the last thing Mama gave her before she passed and before Dalona disappeared and came back in a hospital bed wearing a blue tag bracelet and not remembering much except for Mama and the ladies.

Outside, the sun is too warm and bright for November, a trick sun. Her eyes burn from the glare. Dalona wonders whether she's disappeared and it's spring now. She lets out a breath of relief as she passes a drug store with a sale sign for Halloween candy. No one knocked on her door for treats last night. She hates Halloween. At least Thanksgiving and Christmas, even Easter, bring special meals, turkey or ham and fixings, at St. John's or the Perry Center. All she gets for Halloween are caramels that stick to her teeth.

The clock outside the Mark Twain bank says 10:17. If she hurries, she can stop by the attorney's office and still get lunch at St. John's. Mr. Willis helped her get checks after Mama passed. She liked him fine, though she couldn't say the same for his sister. Dalona wasn't sure what lady Willis did in her glass cubicle. Mr. Willis played Indian music to soothe savage beasts. Dalona didn't believe that and suspected Mr. Willis didn't believe it either. Still, she'd liked the music.

Sometimes when he'd left her in his office alone, Dalona closed her eyes and let the music seep into her. Other days, she paced the room, fingering pieces of Oriental pottery scattered around the office. A jade figure of a woman in kimono, no bigger than a pinky, was Dalona's favorite. She often thought of carrying the little woman with her, hidden in her pocket or clutched in her hand. Mr. Willis had so many other things, he'd never miss this small woman. But she never took it and that was partly why she didn't feel bad when she spent her first check, the big one, on a color TV instead of Mr. Willis's bill. She'd left him the tiny lady which she could've taken easily. That was worth more than a TV. Lots more. Dalona knew it and so did Mr. Willis.

She meant to pay him, still. Every month or so, she brought him five dollars. Brought his sister five dollars, she should say because lady Willis was always the one taking her money. Mister stayed in his office, never bothering to come out to see her any more. But if she strained, Dalona heard faint melodies oozing through his walls, under his door.

"If you made it ten, instead of five, you'd pay off twice as fast, Dalona," lady Willis said last time.

"Can't give you ten because I don't have ten," Dalona said.

"We can all do more belt tightening." Her breath gave off a tiger smell.

The large diamond on lady Willis's right hand glittered as she wrote a receipt. Dalona watched and listened to wisps of music, but didn't say anything.

She fingers the five dollars in her pocket, pleased with the rich feel of it. Wouldn't Mama's ladies laugh at the idea of someone feeling rich just because she has a single bill to fondle? Mr. Willis can wait for his money.

At her bus stop, two men are already on the bench. One holds a small brown sack he raises to his lips, then passes to his neighbor.

The first man lets out a hacking cough after each swallow. "Sure good," he says. He looks over at Dalona. "Hey, baby. You want some? Sure good stuff."

Dalona scoots down her side of the bench until her arm scrunches against the railing.

"Hey, baby. Don't be that way." He giggles. "It's fresh stuff. You can trust the Mick."

"Shut yourself up." She stares straight ahead.

"You looking good, baby, when you be mad. The Mick likes his women mad. Mad with love. Ain't that right, Singer?" He elbows his friend who reaches for the sack and looks surprised when his hand grabs nothing. "Sorry, bro." Mick swallows, passes the sack to Singer, then grabs it back.

Mick is quiet awhile and Dalona thinks maybe he's forgotten about her. Three blocks down the street, a bus stops. Dalona, thinking it might be hers, walks to the curb.

"Hey, baby," Mick whispers to her back. "You know what Mick rhymes with?" He giggles again. "You figure it, baby."

"Shut up, nigger," Dalona says under her breath.

"Oooh. I like my ladies mad. Right, Singer?"

Now Dalona can read the sign across the front of the bus; it's heading to St. John's. The bus pulls to the curb and the doors open, inviting Dalona.

"Hey, baby. Know why they call him Singer? Cause his thing sings like a robin in spring. Sings inside the ladies. Right, Singer?"

Dalona steps into the bus and flashes her pass at the driver. As the doors close behind her, Mick chirps, "Sings like a robin. Sing. Sing. Sing."

She finds an empty window seat where she can watch the outside people who all look as if they're going some place important. Dalona wants to look that way when a stranger behind a bus window spies her walking the streets. She tucks her chin, looks at the floor. Every once in awhile, she peeks out the window, checking herself against the sidewalk folks to make sure she's getting it right.

At Broadway and Twelfth, Dalona reaches up to press the bar which rings a low peal, like a church bell but not so holy, to let the driver know she wants off. All the way to St. John's, she walks with tucked chin, eyes to the ground. She's tempted to glance up to see if anyone notices but doesn't because then she'd lose her look and what she'd see in people's faces wouldn't be true any more.

She's one of the first at St. John's. With the warm weather, the place won't be crowded even by noon. Some days in coldest winter or hottest summer, Dalona would have trouble finding a chair if she got there later than ten. But on a day like today, people don't mind skipping lunch, walking downtown or sitting on a bench instead. Even though the day is mild, Dalona carefully pulls the heavy wooden basement door closed after her. She's heard Sister Helen and Miss Mary talking about heating bills. For free meals, Dalona figures the least she owes is a door shut tight.

"Dalona, dear, good morning and happy feast day to you," Sister Helen says from the table next to the door where she sits folding silverware into paper napkins.

"Morning, Sister."

"How about some help?"

"Sure." Dalona drapes her sweater on the back of the chair across from Sister.

"You're so good with the napkins, Dalona. It shows you have an artistic side, the way you fold the corners just so."

Dalona smiles. Sister likes her. She likes all her guests, but Dalona hopes she likes her special. It's why she takes the bus trip to St. John's almost daily, though the Perry Center is closer. She concentrates on her job, folding each corner as neatly as she can. As guests arrive, she hears good mornings aimed at Sister and a few at her too. But she just keeps working, not wanting to talk for fear she'll mess a napkin.

"Not saying much this beautiful All Soul's Day, are you, dear," Sister says.

"Working," Dalona says.

"That's fine, dear. Just fine." Sister Helen finishes her stack of napkins. "This is your sweet mama's special day in God's heaven."

"I'm not Catholic."

Sister Helen reaches across the table to cover Dalona's hand with her own. "You haven't forgotten your medicine this morning, have you?" She speaks in a low voice as if everyone else doesn't already know about Dalona and her medicine problems.

"I remembered," she says.

"You're sure?"

Dalona stares at her, but doesn't answer.

"Fine. Just fine. I'll let you finish here while I check whether

Mary needs help in the kitchen. Have a lovely Holy Day."

Some days, Dalona is afraid Sister Helen likes her like those ladies had liked Mama. If she passed, Sister'd just find someone else to do her napkins.

She works quickly, not wanting to be stuck sitting with someone she doesn't like. Crazy folks, lots crazier than Dalona, come to St. John's. She doesn't mind long as they keep quiet and mind their own business and just eat. But some of them are talkers. Bits of chewed food dribble out their mouths, foam around their lips along with the talk. Words leak out as if their tongues are faucets with slow drips. They chew and swallow and still the words leak. All those words make Dalona feel she's going crazy too.

Dalona folds the last napkin so the edge limps out like a broken wing. She hides it under the pile of perfect napkins and carries the finished stack to Sister in the kitchen.

"Didn't she do the napkins nicely?" Sister says.

"Always does." Mary stirs a large pot that smells like chicken soup or maybe vegetable. "Thank you, Dalona."

"Welcome," Dalona says. She knows manners. Mama'd taught her. No matter what one of the ladies had given, a piece of chocolate or a scrap of material or leftovers from last night's party, Mama always said thank you. She'd taught her baby to do the same. Dalona gets her sweater, then looks around for a good spot. Next to Emma Barry is an empty corner chair. This being Thursday, Emma's up to four layers of clothes. Dalona glimpses green, brown and purple under pink sleeves. Emma starts dressing on Monday and takes nothing off until the end of the week. She just keeps piling on clothes, one outfit on top of another, so by Sunday she's a round layered bundle of dirty laundry. Come Monday, she strips to bare skin and starts the whole thing over. That's how Emma dresses, winter or summer, fall or spring. By Wednesday or Thursday, Emma smells so most folks won't sit with her. But Emma is quiet and Dalona doesn't mind bad smells.

"Morning," Emma says. "Morning," she repeats when Dalona doesn't answer.

Dalona knows Sister Helen has been reminding Emma to be

Out of Line

friendly so she gives her a good morning back. Dalona likes Sister, but sometimes she gets tired of her acting like this is some society club. Mama's ladies belonged to those clubs, but not Mama and not Dalona and not Emma. Sister Helen doesn't understand that, though, and keeps pushing good mornings and good-byes, conversation at tables. Sometimes Dalona wishes Sister would look around and see St. John's is full of folks who just want to eat and be left alone. But she never says that because she's grateful and knows being grateful means keeping your mouth shut.

Lunch is chicken soup with broccoli, bread, and canned peaches. Every so often Dalona looks over at Emma so Sister can think they're talking and be happy.

"See you tomorrow, I hope," Sister Helen says when Dalona carries her dishes to the kitchen counter.

"Maybe."

"Come early, if you can, so you can do napkins."

"If I can," Dalona answers. She should've just said yes. That's what Mama, who knew how to be just right grateful, would've said. But what good had it done her? Two of her ladies had managed a visit at Truman Medical Center, bringing flowers Mama could hardly see and chocolates she wasn't supposed to eat. A few of them showed up for the wake or funeral, but not one of them came for both and not one of them called Dalona after Mama passed. So there was a limit on how far gratefulness would get you.

Outside, the sun is even warmer than earlier. Dalona leaves her sweater open while she walks, following the bus route because she isn't in the mood for waiting. Sooner or later, she and a bus will arrive at a stop at the same time. She'll get on and know that was the one she was meant to ride. When she remembers, she tucks her chin, focuses on the ground. She is nearly halfway home before she catches a bus.

The apartment feels colder than outside. She buttons her sweater, fastening it with a safety pin where the two buttons are missing, then turns on the set. A game show. Dalona forgets the exact rules. She can't keep one show straight from another, but it has something to do with choice and chance. Make the right choice, take the right chance and you're sitting pretty. New car, stereo, trip to Disneyland. Make the wrong move and you're stuck with nothing, stuck with what most folks live their whole lives having.

The TV people don't do good today. The best any of them gets is a recliner. But Dalona doesn't feel sorry for them. At least they're on TV, really on TV. They got themselves shrunk down until they fit inside a set and now they're happy. Even when they lose, they stay happy. They have no troubles or pain or sorrow. All they have to do is make a few choices. Even when they make the wrong ones, no one gets mad at them or makes them feel stupid.

"Not so much starch next time, Dalona." Or, "These scratches weren't here yesterday, Dalona." Or, "Not enough mushrooms in the salad, Dalona. Get your mama to show you." Mama'd showed her. But Dalona hadn't been able to keep it all in her head, much as she'd tried.

The ladies, every single one of them, had smiled at her mistakes. But when she wasn't in the room, they whispered to Mama. Dalona heard those whispers in her dreams and the whispers said, "Keep Dalona away. Keep her away from us and our beautiful families and our beautiful things." Mama hadn't listened, though. That was the only time she hadn't listened. She kept bringing Dalona, giving her jobs. "They don't want my baby, they don't want me," Mama'd said, but only to Dalona, never to the ladies. Maybe that was why most of the ladies stayed away from Mama's funeral. Maybe they were punishing Dalona and Mama too.

The TV folks didn't have to worry about being pushed out the set if they made a mistake. They just moved to another show, then another, then another. You never found tiny people on the floor next to a TV, thrown out because they gave a wrong answer or did the wrong thing. People in TV were too nice to do something like that.

By the time the last game show flickers off, it's five o'clock. Dalona remembers the trash. That would have to wait now because the wild boys would be out and Dalona wasn't matching up against them if she could help it. Instead, she plucks her nail clippings from the top of the trash heap and carries them back to the sofa where she lines them up by size, biggest down to smallest. She pushes them into the cushion, sharp points digging in like swords. When she has them all standing straight, tiny nail soldiers, she presses her palm gently across the top points, careful not to knock any over. Even the tallest are shorter than TV people, but just as hard. You could hit a TV person all you wanted and she wouldn't flinch. Dalona crawls to the set and shoves her thumb, hard as she can, against June Cleaver's face. June just keeps right on telling the Beaver to wash for dinner. Dalona wishes Mama's ladies had been like June Cleaver—tiny and hard and never angry. That's how Dalona wants to be. She hadn't known until this moment. But now that she knows, she'll never forget. Even if she disappears for weeks or months or years, that would be something she'd never forget. It would be like Mama or her green sweater or the ladies.

Maybe the nails were a beginning. Maybe nails were how all TV people started and soon she'd find herself shrinking, her blood too heavy to flow in an easy stream, her lungs too gummed to hold air, her heart a rock too thick to beat her life. Maybe that's where Mama went when she died, not some Catholic heaven people only bothered with on All Souls' Day. Dalona would study TV people more carefully now. She might glimpse Mama sitting in the courtroom of *LA Law*, in the audience of *The Price is Right*.

She crawls back to the sofa, but stays on the floor in front of her altar of nails and presses a palm against their points again, then plucks the tiniest one. As hard as she presses that nail against her fingertip, she can't draw blood. She sticks it in her mouth and bites. But the nail doesn't crack, so Dalona swallows it whole instead. Though she hadn't planned on doing that, she knows having a rigid sliver growing inside her is right.

Dalona reaches for another nail. Soon, she'll be filled with nails and ready for TV life. Crazy people will leave her alone and Sister Helen will find someone else to fold napkins and Dalona will be free, never worrying or wondering again. She'll drift from show to show, no one caring whether her answers are right or wrong. She might even be June Cleaver some day—tiny and hard and never angry.

Hospice Nursing 102

Belinda Subraman

Today I watered the garden to nurture myself
hoping to ease the swell in my heart
from so many long good-byes.

In these end-of-life bonds
there is always a pang
from having missed out
but an awe for their sharing
their journeys with me.

They show me their accumulated lives
as they tell me the drama of their being.

The depth and sadness of easing
each new friend home
I ignore sometimes
for the pure reward of a good death.
The gravity needs to be aired and let go.
I cannot move if I hold on.

Bereavement care is for nurses too
but we must give it to ourselves.
So today I watered the garden.
It wept with my care and thanks.

Out of Line

BEDELIA

Prudence Todd Moffett

Bedelia sank into her seat, breathless. She looked around the enormous auditorium. She had always considered her church spacious, but it couldn't compare to this. She entered the Kentucky Center for the Arts for the first time, out of breath from mounting the wide stairs. She had hurried the six long blocks from Broadway to Main Street. Now, she showed her ticket to a uniformed lady in the lobby.

"Oh yes. You want the Whitney." She pointed to a pair of doors, where a few people were lined up having their tickets taken.

Bedelia was early, and the magnificent room was filling. White folks, most of them in pairs, slid along the rows, squeezing past the knees and avoiding the toes of those like her who were early. She had plenty of time to straighten her skirt, smooth her sleeves, and make sure her hair was tidy in its bun. She looked with interest at the people in boxes suspended on either side of the vast space, at the unusual bumpy ceiling.

She breathed deeply, let her body sink into the plush. She'd been on her feet all day, pushing herself, so she could come to this performance. Mrs. Thornton's son, Eldred III, had pressed the ticket on her.

"I'm not going to make it to this one, Bee," he said. He was the only one in the family to call her that. She had overheard Mrs. T's bridge group make fun of the name Bedelia.

"Where do they find these names?" one lady asked the rest after Mrs. T had rung her little silver bell one day and told Bedelia to fill the mint and nut dishes. Playing bridge must take a lot of energy, the way those little dishes emptied. The kitchen door hadn't finished swinging to when the woman spoke in a squeak that carried. When it swung the other way, Bedelia heard laughter. They couldn't have known that Bedelia was the given name of a fine white lady her grandmother had worked for. It might be old-fashioned, but that was all. Bedelia pursed her lips. She liked old-fashioned things.

She could tell they'd been talking about her, because the room fell deadly still when she reentered. She placed the pastel butter mints and honey roasted peanuts on the corners, safely out of the way of the cards, and asked whether there were anything else, ma'am. Mrs. T, frowning over her cards, shook her head. Bedelia headed for the kitchen to pare potatoes for the evening meal. This time it was Mrs. T's voice she heard.

"Say what you will about that name, she's a treasure." The door swung to. Bedelia's toe kept it open a crack.

"How long have you had her?" The squeaker.

"Oh, let me think. She didn't toilet train Eldred, that was Mavon. But she started pretty soon after. At least twenty years. Never late to work, except when the buses are off schedule. Snow and ice. You know. But she gets here, somehow."

Bedelia's lips curled. She'd worked all one day with frost-numbed toes. At the time she'd seen Mrs. T staring at her, apparently afraid to ask why she was limping. Bedelia had given up thinking Mrs. T was a jewel. She was restless at her constant demands, though she understood that was because they all depended on her so much. Watching Mrs. T daub ineffectually at a blot of mayonnaise she'd spilled on the floor, Bedelia felt a sense of superiority. What must it be like to be so helpless? No one would ever have to keep Bedelia's house for her.

"She's not one of these fat ones, either." Bedelia recognized the baritone voice of the woman from next door, a chain smoker. "Why does being poor equal out to being obese, anyway? You'd think it would be the other way around, wouldn't you?"

"Keeps herself trim, hair tidy, never a whiff of body odor," said Mrs. T. Usually, all Bedelia heard from Mrs. T was criticism. Could she see the kitchen door ajar?

"Is she married?" asked the squeaky voice.

"Oh, come on girls, let's play," said the neighbor's daughter-in-law, recruited at the last moment to fill in. Bedelia removed her toe.

Eldred had been the same age as Bedelia's Sonny. They had

grown up at the same time, Bedelia caring for Eldred days and Sonny nights. In each of them she saw echoes of the other. Sonny had left home at about the time Eldred had gone away to college. But now Eldred was home again, college graduate, successful writer in a New York ad agency, but strangely pale and quiet.

When he first arrived and moved back into his old room, Bedelia heard muffled shouts from Mr. Thornton's study, where he and Mrs. T were talking behind a door that stayed closed. Mrs. T went around with red-rimmed eyes the first month.

"I wouldn't want to put you at any risk, Bedelia," Mrs. T said. "And I certainly hope you'll stay. I need you now more than ever." Bedelia wasn't certain what all this meant, but Eldred was much tidier at twenty-five than he had been at fifteen, and goodness knows he didn't eat as much. Must have been all those pills he took so regular. She stayed.

"This ticket," Eldred had said when he fished it out of the big envelope he kept all his tickets in, to the orchestra, the ballet, and who knew what all else, "this ticket will give you a chance to see one of your own people. Andre Watts." Bedelia had picked up JET magazine at the hairdressers. She'd read about Andre. Since Eldred was trying to be kind, she kept quiet and tried to look impressed. "He's just great. Plays the piano with the orchestra. There's some other stuff on the program, but he's going to wrap it up. Give it a whirl, Bee."

Bedelia had protested. "I can't take your ticket, Eldred,"

"I want you to have it. Please." So she approached Mrs. T, at first not mentioning Eldred or the ticket. Could she get off early that Saturday. At first, it wasn't convenient, but Eldred overheard.

"Mother, I thought Bedelia would get something out of hearing Andre Watts. How many black classical pianists are there?" Mrs. T raised her eyebrows, and the way she spoke Bedelia could tell that she found something amusing. The Thorntons were like that, always thinking they could hide the way they felt from her.

"Well, I guess I can load the dishwasher, if you'll stay till dinner is ready." She thought a minute. "How about coming half an hour early Saturday morning. Then we'll have the house ready if anyone drops by for cocktails." If Mrs. T had been as alert to others' reactions as Bedelia had to be, she might have noticed that Bedelia found that "we" amusing. Bedelia, however, was simply expected to agree, and she did.

Now the auditorium seats around Bedelia began to fill. She noticed on either side of her good-looking young men, like Eldred. Since she'd almost raised him -- what with Mrs. T's worthwhile Women's Club activities -- she looked for some of the boys who'd hung out with him in high school. Not finding them, she settled and took another deep breath. They even smelled good, like Eldred.

Bedelia remembered checking him, top to toe, mornings before the Country Day bus picked him up at the foot of the drive. Serving him breakfast school day mornings as he grew, she knew the smell of good soap. She'd had to check Sonny early, before she headed out to wait for her city bus, and hope he had the good sense to get on his own school bus when the time came. All six of her children had seen themselves off to school. The older ones helped the little ones, till Sonny's time to start, when the older ones were all gone. They'd lived in a drafty shotgun house. The upstairs bedroom belonged to the boys; the girls were downstairs; she shared the little back bedroom with Sonny when he was a baby.

Working two jobs, she'd missed most of the fun with the girls. Occasionally one of them would be studying late at the kitchen table when she got home from the office building she cleaned. Then they'd talk and laugh till too late for both of them. Mrs. T often scolded Bedelia for yawning.

"Do you know how rude that is, to yawn in front of me like that?"

Bedelia had her own laundry and cleaning to do. The girls took care of the dishes at home, and the boys the trash and yard. And Sunday was Bedelia's day, though she could tell Mrs. T begrudged her that. At least the offices were nice and quiet. No one followed her around.

"I'm just old-fashioned," said Mrs. T. "I have old-fashioned standards."

When she didn't follow Bedelia around, Mrs. T used to sneak

up on her.

"Did you move the dresser?"

"Did you dust all the books?"

"What about the piano keys? Clear to the back?"

When Mrs. T took up tennis, it was a relief.

Now Sonny was gone, Bedelia was down to living in one room, partly because she was only working one job. Nowadays she barely had enough to meet her needs, and was embarrassed when her church asked for a tithe. She couldn't spare it.

On stage, the orchestra filed in. She particularly noticed how the young women's blonde hair contrasted with their black dresses. And the men's dark coats stood out against their gleaming white shirt fronts. Sonny looked like that when he waited table for a big "do" at a country club. Le Roi looked like that when he was ready to play a fancy gig.

Sonny had brought Le Roi home from the club. "He said he had heard all he could stand from me about you, Mama."

Bedelia felt that all the juice had been squeezed out of her long ago by working two jobs and raising her children. She didn't even sneak a peek any more at the bus driver or the older single men who came to church. Le Roi's smooth talk got her back up. Musicians she regarded as worthless, dissolute even. She had no use for him at first. But he persisted. He brought her candy the first time. From then on it was flowers.

"I like the way your face softens up over a bouquet," he said.

She softened up over him, all right. Bedelia thought she made a plumb fool of herself. Mrs. T complained about singing like she had yawning. She kept on cleaning offices, because who knew what Sonny would decide about college. The others had worked their way, but she was concerned about him.

A young man, late, let down the seat next to hers and smiled at her. "I'm a friend of Eldred's. He told me you'd be here."

She smiled and nodded back.

"I'm glad you could use his ticket. This should be quite a night." He smelled good, too.

So had Le Roi. And he felt good. He brought her to life. Pretty soon he took to staying over. Sonny didn't wise up for several weeks, and he only giggled when he came down early one morning and found them together at the breakfast table.

"Why do you work so hard, woman? Sonny's almost done with school. Give it a rest." Le Roi wanted her home weeknights when the band was quiet. But Sonny needed senior pictures, a yearbook, maybe even a date for the prom.

"They need stags too, Mom, if I go -- " It worried her that he was a loner. She would have been scared to death if he'd hung out with a gang, but would have welcomed a girl friend. Still, there was his graduation robe to rent, a trip to Washington.

Le Roi was around the house a lot, days. She could tell that from the ashtrays. She even got used to the sweet smell she couldn't identify.

Musicians were a law unto themselves, Sonny said. "He's tight with his stash. Won't give me one toke."

One Saturday night when she came in late and cold from the bus stop—the Thorntons had entertained—there he was.

"No gig?" she asked, using his lingo self-consciously.

"Sit down, Sugar," he said. "I need to talk to you." His eyes were bright, his movements spastic. For the first time she wondered if he was on something else. "I've got a chance to get in on a money-making deal." He kneaded her neck and shoulders. Ah. That was something that always softened her. "This is something really good. We could be on easy street, darling." His eyes were, if anything, brighter. "I've dreamed for years about a chance like this."

"What is it, Le Roi?" She'd stopped dreaming years back.

"Oh, don't trouble yourself with that. These guys that are cutting me in want it kept quiet. But it's fool-proof. Nothing can go wrong, believe me." His voice flowed like honey.

"What's holding you up?" What could he want from her? "Just some promise-money, Sugar. A few thousand, that's all. A second mortgage on this place would do it."

Bedelia lifted herself slowly to her feet. "Coffee?" she asked and went to the kitchen. She stirred the instant and put in the two spoonfuls of sugar she knew he wanted, and carried their mugs carefully back to the living room. Then she spoke.

"Le Roi, what if I don't have any interest in this house? What if I've been renting it for over twenty years, and it still belongs to Mr. Goodman's Realty Company?"

Le Roi was shocked. "But, you don't rent. Sonny told me. After all these years, you must have good equity by now."

Bedelia had told her children, coming up, that they would always have a place to come to. The sacrifices they had to make were weighed against that comforting assurance. The older ones were all settled now and doing well. There was only Sonny. Somehow her mind was not at peace about him. And here he was telling family business to an outsider, and putting it all at risk.

"Sugar." Le Roi put down his cup. His glowing eyes held hers. "Trust me. You know I'd never do anything to put you and Sonny in harm's way." The tenderness won her over. Of course Le Roi was looking out for them—for the three of them. He talked like they had a future together. She yielded.

"Some bank business," she told Mrs. T, who looked worried rather than mad, but excused her.

"This money better come back quick," she told Le Roi. "Only way I can pay two mortgages for long is to quit heating and eating." Le Roi looked hurt. "It's a sure thing, Baby." She found a fifty-some year old Baby ridiculous, but it felt good, so she smiled. He put his arm around her shoulders and rested his cheek on top of her head. "Everything's copacetic, Baby."

But it wasn't. Unless copacetic meant bad things.

"I don't know how it happened." She hated to see his eyes so troubled, his face drawn and pale. "Those guys that cut me in are just plain gone. Nobody around town's seen them. No forwarding address. Office shut down. For rent sign in the window. Mail comes back. Maybe they'll write." But of course they didn't.

Le Roi was so quiet she couldn't bring herself to reproach him. He had his pride, she knew. But she began to wonder, was that second mortgage on his mind from the first? Maybe you've been a fool, Bedelia, she told herself. She took another cleaning job,

Sundays. The brightness in Le Roi's eyes clouded over, and bit by bit he was less eager for her, less attentive.

In time he was around less. She noticed one day his shaving things were gone. When she hadn't seen him for a week, she asked Sonny if he'd seen Le Roi at the club.

"Yeah, he's still there, Mama. But we don't buddy like we used to." Did she see pity in Sonny's face?

By graduation time, Le Roi was out of the house and out of her life. She began the slow process of shriveling up to less than she was before she knew him.

She straightened the cuff of her sleeve. Le Roi had given her the dress, her good dress.

"Neat, like you are," he said. "Silk, soft like you are."

"That's enough." She had stopped him. She knew in a woman her age more flesh wasn't becoming. But the dress covered up some of the angles of her frame, and she loved the red and green glassy sparkles scattered around the tidy print. She could wear it in winter, but it was light enough for this warm evening in early September.

She'd laid out the dress this morning, knowing she'd be in a rush when she got home. She'd overheard, knowing she was meant to overhear, Mrs. T scolding Eldred for giving her the ticket. It had upset Mrs. T's whole day, she said. Reluctantly, she let Bedelia go at six. Not for the first time, Bedelia wished she had some second-hand jalopy, some piece of junk that she could afford, to take her home.

Mr. Thornton had taken her home once when she'd slipped and sprained her ankle. When she called Mrs. T the next morning, she said to take the weekend, and that if Bedelia did need to see the doctor, Mr. Thornton was sure their insurance would pay for it.

The night of the concert she had hurried up the long staircase to her second-floor room, which she had furnished with the best -- no, the least worst -- furniture left when she broke up housekeeping. She turned on the throbbing little air conditioner that, barely moving the air, by the time she got home would have cooled the room enough to sleep. The bathroom was empty, so she was able to freshen up quickly, slip into her dress, and be on her way.

Now the auditorium was full, all the chairs set out for the orchestra occupied, the audience quieter, expectant. Bedelia read the program. Fanfara, they called this concert, first of the season. Berlioz she was not familiar with. She had heard the name Mozart before. There was an article about Andre Watts, which she struggled through. The light was not bright, and the print was faint and small. Sitting so comfortably, she felt drowsiness creeping over her in the crowded room, in spite of the air conditioned breeze.

The first piece kept her awake. A Roman Carnival must be exciting. But during the long symphony, in spite of herself, she dozed off. The applause woke her. She'd had a good sleep now, she felt, and tried to perk up. Everybody was leaving, she discovered. All the people who had climbed over her to get to their seats were climbing in the other direction now. Would they come back? Or had they had enough?

Eldred's friend stood up to stretch.

"I haven't talked with Ell this week. How's he doing these days?" The smile was gone, his face sorrowful, almost.

"Just quiet. Keeps himself to himself," she said.

"Almost like he's afraid he'll— " The young man broke off. "Maybe I'd feel like that, too, if I— "

Bedelia had wondered how parallel Eldred's life was to Sonny's, and these words heightened her suspicion. Eldred didn't look sick, just a little thin was all. But for a while Sonny too— .

"His friends don't hang out at the house the way they did when he was coming up," Bedelia said. "I've about forgotten how to bake chocolate chip cookies."

"I didn't go to school with Ell," the young man said, "but even I've heard about those cookies."

Bedelia resolved to bake Eldred a batch on Monday. The conversation broke off, as all the people who had gone out proceeded to come back, and Bedelia had to press against the back of her seat and turn her toes sideways to let them by.

Then there was a hush. The orchestra sat at attention, rearranged around a gigantic black piano that had risen majestically from beneath the stage. Then from the little door that vanished into the side of the stage, Andre Watts appeared. Bedelia knew him at once. He was a brother. His skin was in fact a little darker than Bedelia's, she couldn't help noting. But he was beautiful. He reminded her of Le Roi all dressed up for a gig. Would Andre call a concert like this a gig?

As waves of applause filled the auditorium and bounced off the walls and that funny ceiling, Mr. Watts bowed, and bowed again. The conductor bowed to him. The violin players bounced their bows off the strings of their instruments. None of the members of the orchestra were black, but their faces were lit up, looking expectant.

Finally, Mr. Watts sat on the padded bench in front of the piano, which instantly became his piano. On his way down, he flipped his coattails behind him, and they hung like swallow tails over the bench. He and the conductor eyed each other, and the music poured out. Sonny'd played her a tape of Le Roi's combo on his boom box, Le Roi at the piano beating out the tempo. With all these people playing, this was different, almost too much music to take in.

To her dismay, Bedelia felt her eyelids droop. She straightened in her seat, willing attention. It had been a long day, but she had looked forward to this. Eldred had meant this as a kindness. He had loved the piano himself, growing up. Andre Watts was a brother. She took off and wiped her glasses and repositioned them on her nose. The music flowed. In her weariness, she was amazed at the vigor of his attack on the piano. Brahms, the program had said. She blinked.

Andre Watts bent low over the instrument. His whole body partook of the music. It was as much a pleasure to watch him as to hear the sound. He was so graceful, crouched low over the keys in quiet moments, then rearing back and breathing, then bowing his head to listen to the orchestra. She noticed that he kept an eye on the conductor's left hand through it all. How did he do that and play at the same time? At one point he might have been praying, his head bowed over his folded hands. Sometimes when the music called for his hands to run from the lowest notes to the highest, his fingers would run out of keys, slip off the end of the keyboard and droop there, motionless.

In spite of herself, Bedelia slept, soundly this time. She was completely unaware of the music, the room, the people. The harmonies washed over her. The rise and fall of the melodies left her undisturbed. The crescendos that precipitated untimely applause didn't completely wake her. She was with Sonny in her dream.

After he graduated from high school, Sonny had shaken off every suggestion of higher education.

"No, Mama, I've got me a job in a florist shop. It's driving the delivery truck for now, but they said I could come inside just as soon as there's a vacancy. I don't need college to put together a beautiful bouquet." She loved flowers herself and had to admit he might be taking after her, so she didn't fight it.

Almost right away, he moved out. And by the time he dropped by, hollow-eyed and thirty pounds lighter, she was in the second-floor room and had nowhere to put him. They found a place where he could stay, and she visited him every day till the end. And here he was in her dream, a little one climbing up in her lap, patting her cheek.

This time the applause that woke her was thunderous. She could hear people shout something, over and over. Andre Watts was bowing, smiling this time. The tumult went on and on. Will he tire his back with all that bowing, she wondered? He turned to shake the conductor's hand. The two men embraced. How must he feel, all this thunderous roar directed at him? Then he went around the back of the piano to hug the white lady who played a bigger version of the violin, one that stood on the floor. Hugged her, a white lady. And the applause and cheers just got louder. Would it ever stop?

Bedelia felt tears. A brother. She had read in the program that part of his earnings went to help AIDS patients. He looked healthy, though. Could he be like Sonny and Eldred? She had no way of knowing. There was no way of knowing. Her fingers caught the tears on the line of her chin.

Out of Line

    At last the cheers slacked off. Andre Watts left the stage through the invisible door, only to return, three times. When he didn't come back the last time, a buzz of conversation rose as the audience filed out. Bedelia nodded good night to Eldred's friend, stood erect and proud, and went home to her room.

Out of Line

WHAT IN THE WORLD ARE WE DOING?

II

September 11, 2001

Belinda Subraman

My day begins at 4:00 A.M.
A patient has died.
I go to Pronounce.
Humility and compassion is the mood.
The niece stays with me.
We wait for the medical examiner to call back.
We talk. She seems even more polished and kind
the more I get to know her.
She tells me family history, shows me photos.
She asks about me, learns how I came to be a nurse,
that I am divorced but happy
and somewhat fulfilled.
Finally when the mortician comes we hug goodbye.
She adds a kiss on the cheek and I return it.
Intimate, poignant death!
I walk out into the sunlight
feeling depth, satisfaction, compassion.
A young man runs after me
saying something about a bomb.
I say, "Oh someone made a bomb threat?"
"No, the World Trade Center has blown up and the Pentagon!"
"Oh, this is a sick joke isn't it?"
"Listen to the radio,"he says. "They're talking about it everywhere."
Shock, disbelief, unhinging is the mood.
I drive to work puzzled and sore from death.
TVs are blaring everywhere.

Over and over again planes fly into buildings.
Everyone goes home by 2:00 except me.
I'm on duty until the next morning, on call for the dying.
I am alone. I cannot sleep. It's the longest night in history.
There's talk of Armageddon
and 5,000 people disintegrating with no trace.
The shallowness of culture, habit, money falls away.
Nothing is important anymore but love, family, treating each other
    well.
Night passes with wavering uncertainty.
This is the end of life, as we've known it.
It is the end of life as we've dreamed it.
It is the end of the assumption of safety.

———————————————

Detasseling Crew

Wilda Morris

Why did we sit mute
unmoving
on the floor of the truck
stomachs knotted
while a tall girl with ratty hair
held a match under the foot
of the old woman?
Why just watch to see
what the woman would do?

That girl would have fit in
as a guard
in a prisoner-of-war camp.
She already knew
how to torture,
how to steal everyone's courage.

Why *did* we sit mute
unmoving
on the floor of that truck?

White Rice

Melissa Shook

Arms full of hand-woven jackets plucked from warehouse racks,
I wade into the dressing room, too many women trying on garments
from Blanco Negro, Iridium, Colourz, White Rice,
elbowing into four narrow mirrors propped against one wall.
Linda promised to stop me from buying too much,
but "I need" and 'I want" prevail.
Stuffed into a white plastic grocery bag are $154 worth of clothes.
Flushed from the bargains, I relax as my friend drives toward lunch.
The car inches up Harvard St., passing an old woman,
    (maybe my age)
wearing a flat straw hat and fuchsia shirt,
pulling her supermarket cart piled high with black garbage bags
bulging with soda cans. Ahead, a man, in a conical hat,
    clears the way,
shifting boxes standing waist height against the furniture store.
His cart finally free, she follows,
as if they were leading water buffalo across farm land in Vietnam.

Wounded Knee

Bob Monson

They were just waking, some were slow
When we rode in, bright sabers drawn.
Our horses bolted at the embers' glow.

Still we charged on; we did not know
How they would fight in early dawn.
They were just waking, some were slow.

Small children searched where to go
And clutched at their mothers beyond
When our horses bolted at the embers' glow.

Old men brought out shield and bow
Then fell with buck and doe and fawn.
They were just waking, some were slow.

The feel of death with every blow,
Laughed at the blood and the babies gone
When our horses bolted at the embers' glow.

What keeps me steady I do not know.
I hear the rushing fear at dawn.
Some were just waking, they were slow
When our horses bolted at the embers' glow.

To A Case Worker

Sara Littlecrow-Russell

I must have come into your office smiling —
too clean, too friendly,
too well-dressed.

I was not one of the "deserving poor"
the ones who say
"yes ma'am" and "please sir"
the ones who bow their heads
to avoid looking you in the eye
and move quickly out of your way.

I made the mistake of refusing
the welfare department's
vocational training program
which would have spent
two years and lots of tax dollars
to teach me to say
"Do you want fries with that?"
Instead I went to a four-year college
and you made it plain,
scholarship or not,
that I had no business
trying to climb so high.

I must have been
too smart
too hopeful
because you made a paper noose
out of vouchers and forms
and then tightened it
until my future
lay limply suffocated
on your office floor.

Imitation Eagle Feathers

Sara Littlecrow-Russell

For $20.00 I can tie
An imitation eagle feather in your hair
And from a distance
No one would know the difference

For $10 I can sell you a patch
Neatly embroidered with
Confederated Chapter —
American Indian Movement.

For $5.00 I can buy a roll of film
And take dramatic photographs of you
Poised in black angry hat and braids
Against a rented South Dakota landscape

For $3.00 I can stamp your hand —
Admit you through the powwow gates
So you can glower at white tourists
And blonde half-breeds.

You can give me
Twenties, fifties, hundreds —
But feathers, patches, hats, and braids
Cannot make you a warrior.

Midwestern Conversations

Bryan Thao Worra

You're the whitest guy I know,
Nate tells me over a backyard BBQ
At the end of high school.

It's supposed to be a compliment.

You speak English even better
Than some of the students who were born here
A teacher tells me after hours.

And it's true.

I'm pulling you over, sir,
Because frankly, you look like one of the bad guys,
A cop tells me, his hand on a holstered Glock
In Ohio. And you've got an awful lot of cash on you.

But I'm just getting my rent for my landlady
Who doesn't trust my checks!

The other day, a young yonsei sent me a poem
entitled, "I Can Be White."

My heart can't give it an iota of serious consideration,
Although it's entirely possible I'm projecting.

Fells Point

Michael Gavin

Apartment life, no matter how long you've lived it, gets old after three days of isolation within.

Redundant clips of empty, white streets and interviews with three-toothed children with sled or shovel in hand who are happy not to be in school serve as breaking news, although every soul in Baltimore is aware of the goings-on outside because the same blizzard being reported upon is what keeps them inside.

You know the news because you walk outside and see how much snow has fallen. You are in awe that you and your wife are among the only souls out there.

Your wife points out how much nicer things look when they are covered in snow. "It's so clean. Unlike the city. But we're in the city." You both know what she means is that you can't see the garbage, evidence of the total neglect people have for others that manifests itself in the form of paper coffee cups, hamburger wrappers, cigarette butts. Here, in Baltimore, that litter sits like a beard on the dark face of the Chesapeake, and the white covering the water makes this place seem of another country, another culture. Your wife likes this, and she slips her gloved hand through your arm.

You walk down Thames to Broadway, and your wife is happy because there are people digging each others' cars out. There is a taxicab spinning its wheels in the snow. You think to yourself that cabbies ought to be better drivers than to think that by accelerating more and more their cars will miraculously jerk out of the pit there in the snow. But not this cabbie.

Before you part, your wife kisses you and you knock on his window. He rolls down his window and nods. You tell him you can help him if he doesn't mind ruining his floor mats. In his Barbadian accent he agrees. You look up at your wife, the bits of snow falling between you and her. She cocks her head in pride as you slide his floor mats underneath his back wheels and then you lean forward and tell him to ease forward. He does and he is already turning down Broadway. He does not idle for a moment, and he leaves his floor mats in the snow. The yellow cab dissolving into the gray of cold and snow and white ground.

Your wife is troubled. "Do you think you should leave them? The floor mats. In case he comes back?"

"We ought to take them. Not leave them out here."

"But if he wanted them back, how would he ever know who we are? He probably will never be able to retrieve them."

"We could help other people with them. I mean if they're stuck. On our way home. We should take them."

"I guess."

"That's what this weather does for people. It makes them want to help each other."

You bend down and take up the floor mats.

Neither of you asks where you are going. You have done this walk before, and each of you love it for different reasons. Frederick Douglass came to Maryland on the port you are walking on, which is enough to make you love any spot on this earth, and the factories' smoke against the sky, despite color of the night, is what your wife calls beautiful, so you walk Fells Point. Tonight, you have to raise your feet over what newscasters have estimated twenty inches of snow. It is cold. The snow on the ground is perfect and you both ruin it with your footprints. And out there, on the brick peninsula, one hundred yards from any road or restaurant or anybody else like you and her, things are good. Snow falling gently is reminiscent of something distinctly human, something pure, something your wife has more of than everybody else.

When you reach the end of the pier, you place the floor mats down on the ground and turn to hold your wife. You are totally alone out there. When you turn to look the direction from where you came, there is the graying figure coming towards you, but your wife does not see it. She does not think of bad things until they come to her, and so you find it your job to think of them always, for you need her to be safe and this is Baltimore.

She cranes her neck to kiss you and you dip down and kiss her. Then she buries her head into your chest and looks out to the water.

She is thinking that the way snow falls on the water has something so perfect to it that it must communicate something of the way we are all supposed to be with one another: gentle, right, and perhaps capable of dissolving into each other.

But while she watches this, the figure advances.

"Ay you," the figure says. It is a hulking figure and he is carrying something big, something solid on his shoulder.

"Ay you. You have my fla mats."

Your wife detaches herself from you. You want to hold her close, but you know from his tone that he is after something other than the mats.

He is now upon you and you hand him the floor mats. Behind him is the falling snow. Fifty yards behind him are empty restaurants, a street void of drunken banter. Peaceful white. He slaps the floor mats from your hand. They flop on the snow.

He now leans back and maneuvers the two by four he had slung over his shoulder to poke you in the chest. He scowls at you.

"You know I did not come all this way for the fla mats."

Your wife has found her way behind you and her hands are on your back. You feel their warmth through your coat, her gloves. You knew you were not going to buy anything on this trip so you did not bring your wallet.

"Listen. We don't need any of this. Just tell me what you want."

He pokes you in the chest and says nothing. In this place, on this gentle eve, his silence deepens the isolation you feel. You think to yourself that there is nobody in the area who could help you if you needed it. Nobody would hear you scream. And if they did, it would be too late to stop this man from doing you harm.

He pokes you in the chest again.

"Give me what you `ave," he says. He is calm, like the snow.

Your wife behind you is scared. "Just give him what he wants, baby."

He pokes you in the chest. You shrug. Thinking of anything you could give him. You think of all the people you've seen on the news, happy, helping each other. You tell him you already gave him all you had when you helped him with his car.

"You think that was what I need? You think that is enough?"

For the first time you notice he has no coat on. He is out here in his t-shirt. His black skin contrasts with the deep white.

There is no answer to his question. He is irritated. And pushes you further and further with his wood, which means your wife must be at the edge of the pier, must be near falling in.

He is angry now and you are scared. You grab the two by four and push him back toward the street. You tell him to let your wife walk back home and that you will give him whatever he needs. He scowls and snaps the wood from your grasp and he points it toward a bench that is nearly covered entirely with snow. "She stands over there."

"Baby?" she asks, but you merely tell her to move over there quickly.

"Listen, we helped you when you needed help."

"I didn't ask for anything."

"Now you are."

He lowers the wood and is now poking you with force. "You give me what you have. And then I will let you go."

The snow is falling hard now. You let out an uncomfortable laugh and look over at your wife who is cold. Scared. She is so small compared to what is happening, compared to the falling snow. You love her.

You put your hands up and say slowly, "All right. Take what I have." You strip yourself of your gloves first, and then your coat until you are left in your underwear. He has not yet moved.

"What you have. That is what I need."

"Come on."

He reaches back and thwacks you on the head. You stumble to the ground, but do not lose consciousness. There is a deep red against the white snow. Your almost-naked body struggles up. The blood is trickling down the side of your face and is colder than the air.

You are out of breath. "Ok. Ok."

You take your boxers off and you fling them at him. He is evil when he laughs. He takes his time to hang each piece of clothing on his two by four and walks back to the street. He leaves his floor mats on the ground. Your wife is scared and you are naked and cold.

"What are we going to do?" She wraps your cold body with her coat.

"I've got to get back," you say holding the gash on your head. You start moving back toward Thames Street where there are people digging each others' cars out of the snow. When they see your naked legs and your blood falling onto the near-perfect snow, they rush to you. A man takes his coat off and wraps it around your waist. A woman takes off her boots and insists that you put them on. A boy gives you his hat to blot the blood. Your wife holds your hand. And the snow falls deeper, making the jagged edges of cars and street curbs round and soft.

Downsized

Jonathan Barrett

"Capacity rationalization has resulted in consolidation of production, which is necessary in order to achieve the efficiency needed to remain competitive in the market."

In between Sunfresh and a strip mall,
a man rummages through a dumpster
to salvage a few thrown-out vegetables—
smell of wet garbage and rancid meat.

At home, in the kitchen, a small hissing
blue flame feeds the bubbling up of water.
He cuts up raw potatoes, slices
onion slivers, and adds elemental spices.

His daughter sleeps on a soiled
mattress surrounded by newspapers
that catch the frozen fall of wasps.
Helping her bury them—their bodies

bouncing off the copper stained porcelain,
her tears swirling in their salty graves—
he sees himself in erstwhile waters
aching to escape this category of want.

Chocolate

Jonathan Barrett

> "Others again exceed in respect of taking by taking anything and from any source, e.g. those who ply sordid trades, pimps and all such people ... For all of these take more than they ought and from wrong sources. What is common to them is evidently love of money ..."
> –Aristotle, Nichomachean Ethics

A boy lives on burnt bananas,
& yams seasoned with salt water gravy.
Ivory Coast officials call it a *clandestine phenomena*. He is beaten & broken
like a horse to harvest cocoa beans
for *Le Gros*, also known as, *the big man*.

He is strung up star shaped
by bicycle chains & cacao branches—flogged
like flailing awning cloth. Officials prefer the term
indentured labor, while he bleeds enough milk
& sugar to make a pound of chocolate per day—
the pods of flooding blood collecting in the mud,

slowly fermenting with cocoa beans, an oily
residue threads down through the rocky soil.
The boy's decaying dirt hands sun-dry
& bag beans for America—the fruit
becoming Devil's food cake, chocolate crunch bars,
& fudge ripple ice cream—among other things.

Drifters

Jonathan Barrett

A man sitting in a booth at Hardee's
unpacking the contents of his duffle bag:
self-help tapes, a notebook, page after page
of notes scribbled in the margins.
He tells you they are footnotes to his memoirs.

You smile and nod, sprinkle *interesting, fascinating*
on the conversation like salt on French fries.
You buy him a cup of coffee and quote Bible passages:
*Ho! Every one who is thirsty, come to the waters;
you who have no money. Come, buy wine, milk, and honey.*

He fingers dirty rosary beads, purses his lips together
and blows on the brown liquid until it's lukewarm.
Sips rivulets through the small slit in the Styrofoam cup.
After coffee you offer him a ride
to the soup kitchen, the metallic scent of sweat

suffusing your car. He tells you he's hitch hiking home,
mostly eighteen-wheelers and windy highways,
uses scripture to ask for money, *everyone who asks receives.*
You give him a five-dollar bill and wish him luck.
You call him a drifter, or *Jesus knocking*

at our door: a homeless man envisaged as Jesus.
You wait in the parking lot. You want this world.
You want to know what he's going to do next.
You listen to freezing sleet tap against the window.
Wait. Watch as he walks down Church Street—

the way old men walk on ice: shoulders hunched
over, collars pulled tight around their necks.
You follow him to Jiffy's, watch him from behind
a pin-ball machine. He lays a pile of crumpled
bills on the counter, buys grape Mad Dog, GPC Menthols,

a postcard with fireworks bursting above a Ferris wheel.
He stands in the alley and smokes a cigarette:
mucus beading up in the bristles of his beard,
the hem of his jacket held together by safety pins,
ashes falling like snow, his breath like an apparition.

———————————————

JUST THE BOYS

Florence Chard Dacey

It's just the boys at it again
making noise, squealing tires
winning, tying people up
waiting for their mothers
to frown, bang the pots, pout.

Just the boys with their sandbox wars
and fires in their pockets
dying into each other's arms
all over the earth.

Just the boys we loved and hated
on the altars, in the beds
on stages playing to soft-hearted dames

and the little girl, turning, turning
in front of the father.

Just the sons we squandered
to save our cages, our sad painted faces.
And these ghosts in different flags
we stitched and pressed so fine
are just the boys
howling their endless question,

Mother, Mother, won't you let me go now?

Out of Line

A Day on the Mall

Christina Trout

It's Sunday morning on the Sixteenth Street Mall in Denver, getting colder. A storm is moving in. The kids are nowhere to be seen. On the bus, a recorded voice set at crowd volume welcomes us onto the free mall-shuttle, encouraging us to make room for the incoming though we number less than a dozen. The only other sound is the stream of Spanish between two young Hispanic men spoken so rapidly, I can't distinguish the beginning and end of individual words. One of them has a tattoo of a perfectly shaped tear at the corner of one eye. Someone says, "Virgin-Mega store," and snorts as if he's said something ironic. I look out the window. All the store-fronts to eye level are scratched with graffiti or smudged, filmed and shadowed by past spray-painted scrawls that have been chemically erased. The ghost images render the formulaic arrangement of merchandise behind the windows strangely impotent, overly rehearsed. We pass a street cleaner steaming the walks, sweeping his arm rhythmically to capture last night's refuse in a stream towards the gutter. An old black man with a cane sits on a planter holding out a cup. An old white woman with bleached hair wears a practiced look of supplication as someone passes. I catch just a glimpse of her turning towards the wall, spewing curses as we pass. We have all seen this to the point it becomes mundane but with the sun obscured, colors saturate and people seem contained, whole almost, within whatever role they are playing this quiet morning. I still don't see the kids and wonder if, as with most young people, it's still too early to expect them up.

* * * * *

Last weekend it was two o'clock in the afternoon when I found them assembled in the concrete canyon which is Skyline Park in the Mall. It was warmer and groups of them lounged or stood together talking. Some had packs as if in transit but most carried nothing, had probably stashed their belongings somewhere for the day. There were fast food wrappers everywhere until a cop rode slowly by on a motorcycle and they slowly began cleaning up as kids grudgingly might, being asked to clear the table. A young dreadlocked girl sat cross-legged mending the pants she wore with needle and thread. A slight, younger man sat behind her hunched over, journal-writing without pause. At one end of the group, an older, kinetic youth opened a jack knife and played with it while he flipped through a magazine. When he got to the center fold which opened like a tongue he passed it around to several of the girls in the group who seemed to take in the airbrushed, overly pink image without reaction as if it were the morning paper. One young man, big, sluggish, got up and attempted to walk up some stairs but collapsed, stiff bodied, convulsing slightly. After a time, another young man walked over and extended his hand. The stoned kid raised his own hand very slightly and heavily as if he was a planet being slowly swung back into orbit. Once on his feet, he stumbled back into semi-consciousness and rejoined the group. I had come here thinking I would be able to talk to them but I only stood, watching from a distance knowing that at one time I might have come here, or some place like it, looking for my step-daughter.

* * * * *

Saba was fourteen when she ran away. We've only recently been able to talk to each other about it and she'll be twenty-one in a few months. She told me at the end of a recent intense discussion that her life would have been different had she stayed with "the mother, father, brother, sister, food on the table kind of thing" we had offered. Because all I could see in looking back was how she had had that for so long and how we went on trying to provide it after she left, that I felt alienated and ineffectual within any role I had tried so hard to fashion and maintain as a mother. Strangely, what remained beyond any lasting outer expression of "traditional family," were frayed strands, evidence of struggle and sadness. Being a family had not been easy. The argument that led to the event of her leaving through a small kitchen window into a neighbor's yard and onto the freeway not far from the small town we lived in was insignificant. It was over dishes, over attitude. But of course, there was more to it.

* * * * *

Off the bus, I approach a man with a red beard pushing a cart full of aluminum cans. I had seen him from the bus pulling a fashionable red purse from a trash can, handling it awkwardly as men do before putting it in the front basket. I ask him if he's seen the younger street kids anywhere. He tells me he doesn't follow that crowd. He's been on the streets since he was sixteen, some twenty years now, but had hung out with the older "bums." Here he gestures towards the lower part of town near the river. There had not been a community of young people then as now. He's never been attracted to "those younger chicks," he says but knows some of the older men "prey on them." This he says slowly, looking at me out of the corner of his eye, and I get a sense of conflicting lasciviousness and quiet outrage from his tone.

Suddenly, he announces that he has streaked on Coors Field and pulls from a wallet a magazine clipping protected behind tape but ragged edged. It is a picture of a naked, red headed man being tackled from behind by two policemen. He tells me he did it to impress a woman but is now using flyers to try to find her. His story begins to catch on itself, become circular. "It's hard to break into art, too many people doing it," he says, offering me a valid day pass to a local ski area. He describes the significance of the date on the pass and describes in slow, thoughtful language the nonlinearity of time, about the ongoing dialogue in graffiti that is to be broken into like a stream of consciousness, about his attempts to communicate with her in this medium as well. He describes the woman he is looking for as having a rose tattooed on her shoulder and two hearts above either pelvic bone. These he says might also be butterflies, but there is definitely "chez-chez" tattooed above her ass. This he knows.

I finally see a young woman standing in front of McDonalds. She's wearing red-plaid flannel baggies, a hoodie, and a soft canvas hat, frayed at the edges, which bells out from her face and long, dark hair. She has a sucker in her mouth and I wonder briefly if it's a soliciting gimmick for men attracted to that sort of thing. Apprehensive, I duck into an ornate doorway rehearsing how I am going to approach her. I notice the names and titles of the people who have offices in the building and see that they are all jewelers and diamond brokers, yet another tribe. A tall young man asks me rapidly for change because he is trying to get a bus ticket but stops short because I am shaking my head no. I am watching his companion whose tongue is thrust from his mouth like a straw, whose head is flung back spasmodically, who is walking in concentric, rapid circles and whose fingers, held tight before him, are like the wings of captured birds. When the tall youth moves away, so does this boy as if tethered. I look for the young woman who is now talking to another young man and I think they are together. Maybe he is with her, a protector of sorts. I approach him first because this is what I believe about them, that she is in some way selling her body and he is her pimp. I've decided I am going to simply offer them money for their time, for their stories, for helping me understand what has brought them to the streets.

* * * * *

For several years we were a family of five, my husband, his son and daughter from a previous marriage, my daughter and I. By modern standards, we would have been considered poor, though our perception of ourselves was not poor, but struggling. What would have suggested our poverty to us had character; we made the best of our situation. We made our own furniture, our own art, discovered overlooked style in thrift stores and created savory meals from basic ingredients. We decided our only way out of poverty was to return to school and we did, my husband full time with a fellowship and I, part time with a home-based canning business, processing everything from jam to pickles. The small town we lived in was also economically depressed and there were problems in the schools with teenage pregnancy and early drug use that distracted from a learning environment. When it seemed the kids weren't getting what they needed, we pulled them out and home schooled. In addition to scholastics, they were very involved in the food processing business. We bought and sold from a regional farmers' market, so there were lessons in community, sustainability and economics. The kids benefited tremendously from being a part of what proved to be a growing but increasingly demanding business. We were busy and the kids and I especially were very close both in relationship and in proximity. I felt we had successfully faced the challenges of combining two families and those unique to step-parenting. I still claim success.

My husband and I, on the other hand, lacked communication skills, probably the most important component in keeping a family together, especially in times of stress. When Saba began to stay away from home, when the drug use began despite lengthy and open discussion between her and me, I was the one who knew and felt it viscerally, who couldn't handle it. I perceived my role as ensuring the balanced emotional unity of our family, a role I felt to be mine by the very fact that I knew so much about the kids. Yet I experienced our family differently from my husband in ways that were incomprehensible and even threatening to him. So, the night I asked Saba to do the dishes and she gave more resistance than I could handle, I lost it. We fought and my husband came home to find Saba pinned to the ground beneath me. I felt like I was attempting to contain or subdue a "largeness" and impulsiveness in Saba that scared me and which I didn't understand. When I let her up, she ran to her bathroom, shutting and locking the door, where she stayed until her father, in an attempt to force compliance, broke in, put her in her room and spanked her. That night proved a breaking point for all of us. Saba left late that night taking a stuffed animal, few clothes and her make-up bag. She would be gone two weeks before we heard from her that she had arrived at her mother's house 3,000 miles from us.

* * * * *

I approach the young man and tell him I am a writer and that I want to write about homelessness and youth. He is friendly, tells me his name is Chucky though I wonder if it's his real name. It turns out they are not together, have just met, and she hasn't caught what I have asked. I ask her as well and we step into the orange and yellow of McDonalds. I clear a plastic lid and wipe crumbs off a table with my palm as we grab a booth. She introduces herself as Jessica. I notice the carefully applied eye-liner and foundation where she has tried to hide small, red sores on her face. She climbs in first and once I learn that they are newly acquainted, I realize she is somewhat blocked in. We are all locked in, an uneasy alliance.

I ask how they have come to be on the streets in Denver. I am looking at Jessica and she explains that at fourteen she was kicked out of her house because she had a twenty-two year old boyfriend. She shrugs her shoulders. "My parents know where I am," she says, "but I don't talk to them." She is now twenty years old, as is Chucky. When I ask, they tell me where they slept last night, Jessica, in the park and Chucky, in a car. He's always too stoned to finish the required series of TB shots to sleep in the shelter. Jessica prefers sleeping with two male friends. In a shelter, women are separated from the men and they like to stay together. There is an area where security guards let all the street kids sleep and make sure they're awake and away early. There is also a division between the older street folks and the kids so they might not be welcome in the shelters at all. Chucky mentions hearing about an event that happened several years ago when seven homeless men were beaten severely and killed in the mall area, two of them found with their heads severed. Several young homeless males were arrested for it and it was rumored the work of the "mall rats," as the street kids are labeled by some.

Chucky wears a skull cap pulled just above his eyes so he has to lift his head to make eye contact, which he does often and with self assurance. He is coy, flirtatious. His whole family had been involved in Crystal-Meth production in California, his brother "a big time gang-banger." He'd gotten tired of it and had run away, "jumped out of a moving car, got on a bus, like that." He went on to describe how he had been going to night school, had worked as a welder, a telemarketer, and had made 40 thousand dollars last year selling credit card insurance over the phone, "it was a huge scam, maybe you heard from me," he laughs. I begin to doubt his rapid fire enthusiasm. Chucky has only been on the street six months. His face is still clear. Jessica also uses her hat as a shield to duck behind, bringing her hand to the brim and lowering her head slightly when laughing or thinking or looking at Chucky. Her eyes are brown, her face gaunt, sallow for her age, though her youthfulness and prettiness are still predominant, so she seems more self-aware, reflective, even wise than degraded as other older junkies I've known and seen.

What shocked Jessica most when she was first on the streets was the use and proliferation of needles. I caught a glimpse of her small town upbringing in the expressive curve of her lifted eyebrow as she described kids shooting up "in the open, as if it was a normal, everyday thing. After awhile it became normal to shoot up." She pauses as if trying to remember the moment of transition. She tells me she's been clean for a few weeks, that she's on her way to New Orleans where she might get an apartment and go to school to learn auto mechanics. She also tells me that she used to have Hep-C, and I know that her habit has outstripped her youth, that she will probably be dead within 10 years, at the most. It explains her coloring. Some part of me doesn't register the impact of this revelation. I don't ask her any more questions about her disease; I want to believe as she does, that it is something she can leave behind. Jessica claims she hasn't had to prostitute for money, that the primary source of income is panhandling. No one she knows in Denver prostitutes. I ask them how they are treated, if people are friendly. I am surprised when Jessica tells me that people are generally nice. I'm surprised because of the general tension or reluctance I feel when faced with someone asking me for change, especially someone so young.

There is something that always remains unsaid, a gulf that I can't quite negotiate. I wonder why she might not sense this anxiety or the same distance which I assume I'm not alone in feeling. I realize she is perfectly comfortable within the constraints of the streets. It becomes clear to me that if within society, we identify people living out their lives on the streets addicted to drugs as a problem, then we as concerned adults, need to be the ones that make the effort, suggest alternatives. The kids are in many ways acclimated to their environment, whether it's beneficial or not. As Jessica says many times in illustrating her attempts and failures to get off the streets, "it's what I know." She talks about a friend of hers who has recently kicked the habit and is working as a cook. "He still drinks," she says, "he has to, to stay clean, to keep his balance." I ask if he still comes around. Chucky asks if she hits him up for money. "No," she says almost reverently, "I wouldn't do that, I support what he's trying to do."

As we talk about the economics of the streets, they both get philosophical, political. It's something they all talk about, discuss. "If there was a needle exchange program, it would take care of crime," Jessica says shaking her head, making a sound from deep inside her gut, "An addict will do anything for a fix. It's physical, you don't know what you're doing when your body needs it."

As she says this, I remember Rick, someone I had known who came to an intentional community where I had lived for a short time. He was addicted to heroin and wanted to go through withdrawal in a safe environment. He was fine for about three weeks and then started using again. One night he built a fire in a hay field, wrote a suicide note in his journal and shot-up with both heroin and bleach. He nodded off, falling forward into the fire, burning three fingers off of each hand. He didn't die because the bleach container he had found in the laundry room was filled with water. He was a gifted guitarist who had played with well-known bands and loved music passionately. It's a powerful addiction and I understand that what she says is not just an excuse. There is exacerbation in her tone, she wants to quit.

They discuss what it will take to get off drugs. Chucky admits needing help, "a kick in the butt," but sees that the desire to quit comes gradually. "Like the alcoholics say, 'one day at a time.'" I find it ironic that he applies this mantra to the process of desiring to quit. Jessica disagrees immediately, telling him it's a sudden realization. It happened to her having left Denver for a few years and coming back to find her friends doing the same thing as before, "shoving nails up their noses for money." She's fed up. When they talk about the pressure to use again, Chucky tells me he "feels vulnerable around people." If someone were to offer him some new designer drug, he'd take it. "There might have been two times in a hundred where I've turned something down." Jessica admits that she too would not be able to turn heroin down if offered.

They both have committed felonies, his, grand theft auto, and hers, dealing, stolen identity, and theft. Chucky is on the run. I think about him sleeping in someone's car again tonight. Jessica committed most of her crimes in California and is fine as long as she doesn't return there. "In San Francisco, it was easy to make money and find occasional shelter," she says. One could "buy a lid for forty bucks on the Haight and sell it for eighty, get a motel room for twenty five." San Francisco used to be the place where she "touched base," but now Denver is home. "So, how about you?" Chucky asks suddenly, "tell us something about your life." I get the sense that he's asking for a show of legitimacy, and when I talk about my writing, it sounds flat, ambiguous.

I tell them instead about Saba. About the fight. How she had run away at fourteen and had made it to her mother's house, before running away again, to Seattle and eventually on her own with friends. I tell them she had gotten in trouble too, having written bad checks totaling over 2,000 dollars in a month's time. I tell them that soon after, she returned home to her mother and was diagnosed as bi-polar but refused to take anything for it after the first attempt at medicating exaggerated her symptoms. They both nod their heads saying they know some kids like that. I want to tell them more stories about Saba, about her slow persistence in finishing high school, in paying back her debt, in overcoming depressions and moderating highs, but I don't. There is a silence. I look past Jessica to see coated forms of people with cups of coffee before them—silent also, like sentinels. "Where is she now?" Jessica asks. I tell them she's joined the Army, that she almost got kicked out of boot camp for flashing some recruits, but seems to be sticking with it. I tell them she has gotten good at balancing herself. She's gotten through the hardest part.

I touch Jessica's arm. I want to make contact, as something feels unfinished, but it's just the formality of goodbye to get through, which arrives stiffly, awkwardly. Jessica heads for the counter to get something to eat with the money I have given her. Chucky heads outside. Back out on the mall it's cold. The sun is already behind the buildings and it's snowing. By the time I pass Skyline Park, the snow has blanketed the city. There is a group of kids huddled together, and I recognize the boy I'd seen earlier, his head thrown back poking the air with his tongue, his fingers rapidly filling the air with invisible graffiti. It seems as if he is transcribing all that's being said by those pacing and animated around him. I'm thinking about Jessica. I want to know more. I will look for them when I am here next among faces that are becoming familiar, but she will be in New Orleans, and I don't expect to see Chucky because he seemed to be here, mid-flight. I wonder if they will be cold tonight.

This Is What Democracy Looks Like
Courtney Lea Franklin

Out in the streets I stand with the people
drenched in sweat, chugging water from plastic bottles,
bandannas tightly knotted over our heads and faces.
We chant in waves of echoing unity.
Thousands of faces smooth with hope and optimism,
others crinkled with life's weariness and day to day survival.
Picket signs bounce, banners sag and tighten
denouncing corporate greed and immigrant sweatshop labor.
Our fists cut the stagnant humid air in defiance and determination.
Swarms of white crosses hover above the crowd,
one for each dead immigrant who dared cross
the *Gatekeeper* of the US-Mexico border.
Who dared seek a better life without the proper paperwork.

Three rows of police fill the sidewalks in blue-black intimidation,
helmets and face shields pulled tight over their tender skulls.
White knuckles eagerly grip heavy black sticks.
Helicopters whip the sky above our heads into frenzied whirlpools
of intolerance,

as armored trucks push us further down the streets of LA's garment
    district.
They've come for a riot; *we've* come for the revolution.
We march on past the human barricades,
sucking in August air, thick with smog and aggravation.
I think to myself, *this is what Democracy looks like.*

Brown solemn faces of garment workers hang above the chaos
from high-rise windows encased in prison bars and wire mesh.
A banner towering at the front of the mass exposes
Old Navy, Banana Republic, Gap as sweatshop whores.
Hidden in the damp waistline of my own pants is a tag stamped
    Old Navy.
I arch my neck backward, the thick lump of shame collecting in my
    throat.
I lock eyes with theirs, stand suspended in the crowd, unable to
    look away.
They wave t-shirts like freedom flags from within the eerie dimness,
where callused hands toil endlessly over clothes, shoes, backpacks,
slaves to our blind consumption.
We shout in hoarse dehydrated urgency,
Obreros Unidos!
beckon them to join us, plead for them to strike.

A woman clad in a pink smock, leans from a 10th story window,
her plump fist shoots upward with ours,
ducking back in before her boss catches her from the shadows.

I'm standing in an American street, in an American city,
Staring up at twenty story American buildings,
Filled with thousands of American sweatshop workers.
I think again to myself, *this is what Democracy looks like.*

On Strike

John McBride

Over ice-choked lots, over the frozen, jutting
Tops of beer cans and scattered refuse from
Clandestine pick-up trucks, they move
In disorderly lines and signs-
"Unfair,""No Out-Sourcing," "No Scabs."

We cannot identify their leaders. There are no
Dashing majors, no intent bird colonels.

Cable and telephone were the first to go,
Then, heat and light.
To be seen at food pantries is the cachet of disgrace.
At school their children get into fights,
They run away from home.
You could hardly expect them to act like
An invincible horde out of Sergei Mikhailovich Eisenstein.

Now they have reached the perimeter,
Sending forth wary glances from the artillery
Of their bodies only;

Now they are at the outer parking lots,
Peering, not through the scopes
Of assault rifles—

Like blindfolded
Justice they look toward
The vanished faces of managers;

Before them, methodically,
Up and down, up and down,
Snowplows scrape away
A Russian winter.

Edward Teller, Father of Nearly Nothing

John Bradley

Oppenheimer, Oppenheimer, isn't that the opera where everyone dies at the end? he once told Yogi Berra. At the University of Leipzig, he studied the physics of the leaping abilities of fleas. He toured the country briefly with his folk group *Strategic Defense Initiative*, which later became *Brilliant Pebbles*, a metal band. At the University of Chicago, he studied the physics of pan pizza. The first megaton H-Bomb was exploded in 1952, he joked, at the same moment Marilyn Monroe was washing a pair of her stockings in a small sink. In 1919 his native Hungary forbid the use of wood burning box kites. Teller once made Ronald Reagan laugh so hard that fragments of sternum had to be removed from the President's colon. Then he would pull out his stopwatch. I deeply regret the deaths and injuries that resulted from the atomic bombings, he wrote in his memoirs, but my best explanation of why I do not regret working on weapons is a question Who's your daddy? For breakfast, an old tie, a few chess pieces, and some freshly squeezed garlic. I am not the father of the H-bomb, Teller often stated. I am a conductor of lounge music as played on coconuts by a band of highly trained and highly gifted gorillas. Teller was born in Budapest, the city where one half never shaves and the other half spends all day and night shaving. With a piece of string, a forceps, and two drum sticks, he could make a three year old understand nuclear fruit flies. In secret interviews with the FBI, Teller revealed how to make boiled cabbage taste like black bean soup. Then he would pull out his stopwatch. His wife, Mici, could be seen erasing the zeroes in his equations and replacing them with tiny drawings of pipes and birds, carrots and hailstorms. Some say this was a reminder for Teller to occasionally take a bath. At Lawrence Livermore Laboratory, he developed a severe allergic reaction to chalk dust, which he never publicly admitted. In 1941, on the day Teller and his wife became citizens, they bought a camera and made a short pornographic film, *Forty-Three Point Seven Seconds*, now worth thousands of dollars. A bomb is the glue of peace, Teller stated at a Colorado State University lecture. The bigger the bomb, the stronger the glue. According to friends, he would steal the salami from Enrico Fermi's sandwiches, glue the two halves of bread together, and then pull out his stopwatch. No one in California currently going by the name of Edward Teller would say he was the father or son of the deceased Edward Teller. In Livermore, a small fire erupted in a private aquarium. No symphony should ever run for more than one minute, Teller said, pulling out his stopwatch, thus bringing to a quick close every concert he attended, often to standing ovation.

Out of Line

THE MONETARY NEWS

Tom Whalen

It accumulates, and it fades.
Today the market killed a million or two
In Indonesia, maybe even you.
We watch the board blink on, and then we raid.

It accumulates, and it fades.
I've learned to take the dregs at the end of day,
Then scrape them in my cup before I pray
Not to be delivered a monied man to Hades.

It accumulates, and it fades.
Dank in his cave, Fafner squats on his load.
Electronic digits are what I hold.
I know to the decimal what today I've made.

It accumulates, and it fades,
Like the day's news left too long in the sun
Or the memories of what we once thought fun.
Why is it now I'm constantly afraid?

It accumulates, and it fades
Away, as if in a dream a fly ball
Soars over my head down an infinite hall,
And before I know it the game has been played.

It accumulates, and it fades,
So I drill my desires deeper into the earth.
Time for us to resettle in Ft. Worth
And strategize our next raid.

A WORLD GONE MAD

III

A Child Must Be Taught

Steve Larson

A child must be taught of times, struggles other than
her own hard dance in her dark eyes. How and when the moon
became a slogan, convinced mothers to sell sons.

How and when this rattler became wedged
in the woodpile, there by the door, where the people
have lined up tired, with their clean empty plates.

If not, how will she know the sound of boot heels
at the door, smell the smoke of her village burning?

Hear the ponies galloping upstream through
the sunrise, the sabers rattling?

The law of the strawberry might be enough:
send runners, bear fruit,
send more runners . . .

THE COAT

Kristin Camitta Zimet

Brawn and bravado, nearly grown,
my son still brings to me
his coat in need of mending—
that long black leather,
tailored nape to ground,
sign of his smoldering and singular
stalk into manhood.
He holds up the hurt place
as children do, so I can make it right.

Where his fist rammed
the pocket, seven layers flap:
the inner cloth is bruised,
the weave so thin, I have to cut it short;
the welting hangs; two leather swatches,
soft as new skin, shiny as baby fat,
lie loose over the body of the coat,
above the slippery lining, held
by ligaments of leather, bony snaps...

Hugging his coat to me, heavy and cool,
I think how war will fling aside,
limp as a coat, a soldier young as he;
and how the body of the earth
rips as we fight on it, shearing apart
from parent rock up to the sprouting skin;
and how the body of our trust
in one another fails, the layered listening,
the patterning of generations gone,
and hope in tatters.

Out of Line

Time I began to take them all
into my hands, choosing a needle
stout enough to thrust
but not so wide it ruins what it sews,
and not so thin it snaps;
choosing a thread that's stout enough
to keep a lasting grip,
but not so thick the seam becomes a scar,
and not so thin it sloughs off
as the fabric holds it back.

I pray as I sew,
making my way among the layers,
slow, sorting out what belongs
together, what must not be bound,
keeping one hand beneath
to ward the needle off,
where he must stride in freedom.
Backstitch and running stitch,
retreat, advance. My fingers blister
with the pull.

God, give me skill to mend
for him, for children everywhere.

YARN FOR BOSNIA

Kristin Camitta Zimet

Some nerve-jangled imp or claw-hook cat
turned these hanks that lay smooth—
gray lambs, bassinet babies, risen loaves—
into a snarl that spills over the table,
smoke curling thick over a ruined town.

Women in Bosnia, pulling free
out of the wreckage lives tangled and split,
bits of blanket and mangled coats,
rolling the ruin up, as women do,
ask us for yarn. For them I begin

rewinding what I have, making a wad
the size of a newborn fist, dancing it back
out of loosening knots, upgathering
into a soft globe, moving the overlap
so that it spirals out, the center everywhere.

Out of this skein my mother knit
an afghan my grandmother held,
white doves against gunmetal grey,
a coverlet for comfort as she died;
her fingers hugged the loops,

her family intact, one generation
snugged into the next, the long yarn
without hitch. Sisters, tie on your lot
to mine. I want to hear your needles
click, counting, casting on.

General Store in Wartime

Maureen Tolman Flannery

It was warmer for him in the general store
with the fire burning in the Franklin stove.
He left his buckle-rubbers by the door.

He came to meet with cronies who had more
time than tasks to keep them on the move.
The air was warm inside the general store.

Their thumbs tucked into overalls they wore.
Their dogs stayed in the backs of trucks they drove.
Their buckle-rubbers lined up by the door.

They talked a little of the one good war
and what the hell were we now trying to prove.
Stale air churned there inside the general store.

The Daily News lay open on the floor
its headlines bleeding into tales they wove
while buckle-rubbers waited by the door.

He said he had to go to do some chores.
This boy's last letter said their squadron moved.
He left the warm air in the general store
put on his buckle-rubbers and closed the door.

Out of Line

KNOWING THE BOMB SO WELL
Patricia Monaghan

After the nightly news and four martinis
he quietly begins to draw the inner workings

of the bomb, knowing the explosion needed
to ignite fission does not itself comprise

the real event; how compartmentalized the bomb,
of necessity, is, to keep the elements

separate until it impacts on target;
with what care the bomb is timed so that

from the moment of release it proceeds
inexorably to detonation.

It is necessary then to explain his drawing
in detail to the children, before they go to bed.

After a few moments he quizzes them:
What are the proper names of the bombs dropped

on Nagasaki, Hiroshima? Who captained
the Enola Gay? How does a prisoner

of war answer the enemy? The children
do not speak. They know release has occurred,

the elements are colliding, impact is inevitable.
It is always a first-strike situation. Always.

GEOGRAPHY LESSONS
Patricia Monaghan

How I learned my world:
born six months after Hiroshima,
learned to speak with names
of Bolovogue and Limerick,
Augrim and Vinegar Hill,
lost battles in a lost land;
learned to read on father's letters
from Japan as he bombed
Pusan, Inchon, Chosin;

celebrated ninth birthday
the day Churchill begged us
not to use A-bombs to defend
Quemoy and Matsu;
celebrated tenth birthday
practicing duck-and-cover
in case the Russians came.

How I learned my world:
battle after battle after battle,
Saigon, Hanoi and Cuba,
My Lai, Khe Sahn,
Pleiku, the Tonkin Gulf.
Now Basra and Tikrit, Kirkuk,
Umm Qasar, Najariah.
Seoul again, and Panmunjon.
Nablas, Ramallah, Hebron.

This is not the way
I want to know my world.

Out of Line

In west Iraq there is a town.
Only one road leads to it.
It is too far from any oil
or water to be important.
I do not know its name.
So far it has been overlooked.

A woman lives there,
a widow my age.
She has dark eyes.
She has a garden.

I know there is a town
like that. I know
there is a woman
like that, in that town.

This is my wish for her:
That she name her own land
and its familiar hills
in words I never know.
That she live and die
safe in its severe beauty.

This is my wish for her:
that I never hear of her.
That she never hears of me.

Quilting Towards Armageddon
Kristin Berkey-Abbott

We quilt towards Armageddon,
stitching together a cover
from cold warrior clothes
that never fit us well the first time:
old policies, old advisors, all the old
nuclear nightmares that leave us
shivering
under the blankets.

FORGETTING

David Radavich

War is not part of our memory.
It's something we do to others, to make
them memorize suffering which
we give to forget.

We do a lot of burying–only
now it's cremation: cleaner, simpler.

The ghosts of others
are not ghosts for us.

To live in the present,
to consume and satisfy
bodies, is to wash away time.

Only the rivers know
what we have killed, what
we have forgotten

hurrying against stones.

Peace is so much harder than war
Alice D'Alessio

Maybe you thought it would be easy
like crossing your fingers, squinching your eyes
and making a wish; or it would arrive
on your doorstep like a gift, wrapped in dove-
embossed paper, tied with pink ribbons.

Maybe when you stitched messages on thick
clean squares with flowers and poems
and hung your quilt in the corridor, you thought
everyone would understand. And the songs –
full of tears, full of hope, would heal.

Maybe when you streamed up State Street
like a river of prayer, with the kids
and the Grandmas, and all your friends
touching elbows and shoulders
waving your signs and chanting *No More War*

you thought the strutting cocks
would slink away, disgruntled
the greed and hate dissolve like jello;
you'd fling open the shutters to a field new-sown.
Keep listening. You may hear the small seeds stirring.

Prayer as Tanks Slouch Toward Baghdad

Judith Sornberger

A refugee from CNN tonight,
I seek sanctuary in this monster
bookstore that has swallowed
whole so many smaller ones.
Yet, like Jonah,
many a story lives on
in its belly.

I am here because the war
has swallowed my son,
and touching paper is the next
best thing to touching skin.

Hear my prayer for human skin,
the one I write across this hand-
made paper, my felt tip stumbling
across crushed flowers.

Beside me a blonde girl caresses
the contours of her cappuccino
as a dreadlocked boy tells her
of the Nile—his voice ancient
with wonder. I pray for the tender
petals of fingertips—hers
that I can almost feel burning

to cross the distance to his face,
their voices flowing
me into other rivers—the Tigris
and Euphrates whose names reporters
invoke every broadcast, names

I never heard till seventh
grade, in a room on a flat prairie
cradled by two other rivers,
Mrs. Wiltse's voice crooning
cradle of civilization and my writing
the words because I liked
the way they sounded.

I'm praying now for a body
I imagine in a distant cradle,
for arms that lift and carry it,
folded close, under stars toward
the river that inscribes the border
between there and hope.
For the crazy quilt of skin
covering this planet.

Sometimes I believe that our skin
holds you to this world the way
the first gold crocus holds the eye
to color, the way our children's
lives hold us to pain. The way
the river must believe it is
the broken vessel of the sky.

RAGING GRANNIES

Shirley Powers

Described in local newspapers as
"a choir of elderly women belting out
Make peace instead of war"
we stand on stage facing
250,000 cheering anti-war protestors
in San Francisco
Two dozen Grannies over sixty
wearing sunbonnets covered with
brightly colored crepe paper flowers,
long skirts and fringed shawls
The crowd roars approval at the
end of each song
We call out "What do you want?"
They answer "Peace"
Waves of applause dance in the
sunlight and though I have no
illusions of being another Janis Joplin
I feel like some kind of aging rock star
so anonymous
so personal

THE FIELD ARTILLERYMAN
Shirley Powers

He appeared on local TV
said he was trained in artillery
was told to "hit the ragheads with
all the ammo you got, and if they're
still coming hit em with nukes and
watch em glow"
He related how he refused to go
how he sat handcuffed on the tarmac
as his troop plane lifted off
for the Gulf

I will remember his story
How one man alone on an airstrip
said "no"
I will write it on my Grandson's
bedroom wall
Age two is not too young
to learn the meaning of bravery

War in the Garden
Carol Pearce Bjorlie

Protected by their marigold infantry,
the *Martian Giants,*
tomatoes of war
rear their arrogant heads
and threaten to unleash
weapons of mass destruction.
Red globes of bombs
thunk in the night garden
shocking
awing
the Asian Eggplant
an elegant
streamlined
engine of fruit
determined
to hold on
to its
beauty,
refusing
to fight,
dangling
instead like
a love-
infused
organ.

Out of Line

THE LAND BETWEEN THE RIVERS

Carol Pearce Bjorlie

> *And we are here as on a darkling plain*
> *Swept with confused alarms of struggle and flight*
> *Where ignorant armies clash by night.*
>   Matthew Arnold, Dover Beach

In this ancient beyond,
birthplace of language, religion, and original sin,
the night wind furls shepherd's robes into desert blooms.

the sky is a grating roar,
the tremulous cadence shows between bombs,
then sand and shrapnel is flung like ocean spray on a beach.

The hungry armies,
not so much ignorant as young,
blow through the city of Abraham's birth,
through the city Jonah didn't want to visit
and at night they write from the ruins:
> *By the rivers of Babylon we sat down and wept.**

*Psalm 137

THE BUILD-UP

Adam D. Fisher

There in the border-land between
the water and the high ground of oaks
and fields, a stand of cedars huddle
like men in bulky overcoats, sway
in early evening westerlies as if shifting
weight from foot to foot to keep
warm while looking
across Conscience Bay at gray clouds
coming from the west like a great armada—imagine,
imagine flags flying, sailors on deck in full
parade dress, while we in our reviewing stand
watch, our women full of pride and protection,
our men feeling full of adventure, the beat
of battle blood, forgetting
the stench of rotting flesh, bodies blown
so fine there's only a finger, a scrap of skin,
a bit of brain for the body bag.

Today, the sky is clear, as if with sleep,
yesterday's fantasy floated away,
the armada mere clouds but we
are still blind to what is yet to come.

Repentance

Brent Christianson

"... *Jesus Christ, because he changed my heart*"
— G.W. Bush

I can not recognize your Christ
dressed in armor, he looks like Mars
holding your horse's reigns
handing you a shield.

But I think I see his body
lethally injected
on cruciform tables in Texas.

I can not recognize your Christ
sitting like a household god
by your front door jamb
protecting you from spirits.

But I think I see his face
in photos of soldiers
and those who were obedient unto death.

I can not recognize your Christ
standing beside you gazing
down at warfare's victims
able to see nothing.

But I think I see his blood
flowing from war wounded
hands and feet, heads and sides.

I can not recognize your Christ.

The Poet During War

Joseph Ross

the wordless poet
is good
for nothing
but stacking bones
into piles

brittle bones
piled high as the
victims
of every century

the wordless poet
stacks bones
perfectly

Quicksand

Joan Payne Kincaid

> I urge the President's own party
> To warn him about the quicksand
> He asks America to wade in.
> Senator Robert C. Byrd, Sept. 17, 2003

They are coming for us...breeding fear,
the store/ the company/ the deranged patriots...
secret *snitches, sociopaths* the *new* thing to be;
go to jail where widening walls separate the innocent;
no lawyers for trials, *tags in your* under*pants* for tracking!
seize grab shock awe weapons of increasing atrocity;
steel doesn't just fall like *that*~ nor plaster puff out like demolition;
after 911 the smell of people cooking
entered our window, a stench that lingered for months;
corporations and government lock in secret manipulation...
donations for and decisions by the *ruling class*
as jobs go south and east in no bid scandals
and big brother destroys the country with a deficit growing daily;
massive job loss continues here while we *re-build* abroad
like a child's knocked down lego tower,
that which was *excellent* before,
historically *irreplaceable*...magical places like the Casbah!
Kickbacks kickbacks...purveyors of weaponry and stolen contracts;
colonizations for Empire learned from ancient Rome,
frauds in current combat;
wealthy and petite bourgeois suburbanites sign-on Humvie
    waiting lists...
false generals hammer down expressways of pretend battle;
people lose homes in economic collapse;
children sell themselves in US streets while a selected president
    prattles
disgrace of *sex tourism abroad;*

people were in denial and pain when a mayor sold-off
steel (possibly containing human remains) *fast* for profit
tampering with evidence never investigated...
the fix is in for war war war.

THE OTHER SIDE

Joseph Gastiger

They must know the war is lost because the palaces are burning, and every call to prayer subtracts a road. A shore of palms along a creek. Another friend. *Salaam*, Abir, who sold pistachios, and stacked a shed with broken wheels. Sumehra, who loved sweets, and read the stars. Tomorrow's horoscopes say nothing of blue bottle flies, grown fat on blood. The dressmaker, Nafi. The barber's wife. The crows must know the war is lost because the palaces are burning. A bakery. A laundry. A souk. The barber's body, smoldering, hisses like water boiled for tea next door as banknotes in his pocket turn to ash. Here's what he saved for—quick Hadiya, in her orange and gold party dress, sprawling beside a donkey, at a bridge. Nobody waves to welcome liberty and polio, and through the smoke, gum-chewing brothers of the far unseen.

WORDS FOR THE ABANDONED

Joseph Gastiger

If you were important, you would be somewhere
else. All the important people have flown away,

leaving their paperback romances folded on chaises
longues by the pool. All of the dignitaries and starlets

disappear moments before the explosions, gone
with their cell phones and bracelets and spice

colognes. If you were blessed as they, you, too,
would vanish—you, too, would wave down a taxi

in Santa Fe, just as the jets release. You, too, would find
yourself weeping to *Giselle*, as soon as tremors hit.

If you can hear me now, you've been appointed
no one to worry about—hiding in a cellar,

coughing in a clinic, crouching in what, yesterday,
could have been a laboratory, could have been a school.

Long after this war ends, before the next one,
someone in medals will lift up an urn of your ashes

and howl for blood. He won't be your child, bitter,
or crippled. Choices were made. You weren't counted.

Thirteen ways of looking at Baghdad

Sean Lause

I

Among twenty Iraqi villages,
The only moving thing
Was the eye of a crosshairs.

II

I witness three crucifixions:
The thirsting earth,
A dead private from Ohio,
His blood seeping through a comic book.

III

The helicopter whirled the autumn winds.
It was a small part of the pandemonium.

IV

A man and a woman
Are one.
A corpse in New York
And a corpse in Baghdad
Are one.

V

The general:
"I do not know which to prefer,
The beauty of fear,
Or the beauty of wounds,
The bullet whistling
Or just after."

VI

A young mother:
"When I died,
I saw the eyes of God
Were made of barbaric glass."

VII

Oh thin men of Baghdad,
Why do you imagine freedom?
Do you not see how the dogs of war
Feed on the bones of your women?

VIII

I know noble accents
And lucid, inescapable rhythms;
But I know, too,
That eloquence is involved
In every murder.

IX

When the helicopter flew out of sight,
It marked the edge
Of one of many wounds.

X

At the sight of the children
Crying in the red midnight,
Even the whores of war
Cut themselves on stones.

XI

Rumsfeld rode over Iraq
In a glass hearse.
Once, a joy pierced him,
In that he mistook
The shadow of his equipage
For a god's.

XII

There was darkness at noon.
It was raining bombs,
And it was going to rain.
The vultures squatted
On our severed limbs.

XIII

A jar in Tennessee
Is only a jar in Tennessee.
Death
Has no eternal form.

Once upon a field

Richard Levine

Once upon a field I sat
a soldier, running the bores
of rifles clean, to forward
the truth of each bullet's lethal path.

Out of Line

I was young and lean,
and trained in the history
of sanguinary verbs.
In causeless war I fought

in boots and rotary wings.
And I don't feel the need to march
in parades or visit graves,
to appease the inescapable

faces of forever-boys
I knew and helped bury —
now mere names beveled
in black, and etched

in the monument war made
of me. And I will not stand
beside adults my children's
age, introducing their children

to the cold stone kiss, and by silence
will to them the lies of war's
noble aims, for I'd want them to say
something painful and true,

something unsentimental to cut
through the pageant of flag shrouds,
gun salutes, and proud words, something
to reveal the body bags and polished

wood caskets that never could hold
the absence of survivors. I'd want
them to say something that might
untrain their grandfatherless child,

something like: *That's my daddy.*
He gave his life to build this wall.

Buchanan at the monkey house
Michael Casey

they left the baby in the field
but they brought in the nursing mother
operation sabre snatch
brought in civilian internees for interrogation
lucky woman got the first chopper ride free
woman is hurting and crying and holds a match
under an empty C ration can
but Clark figures it out
  she wants hot water
and Clark is away getting the water
and Buch says something really crude
about him and her
and Clark returns and Buch
doesn't say anything to Clark
but Buch is still laughing just the same
and Clark goes
  you obvious don't know when
  shut the F up but
  I'm telling you man
  now a good time

A WORLD VIEW

IV

Mr. Yamamoto's Painting
Deborah Miller Rothschild

For as long as I can remember, Mr. Yamamoto's painting hung in my parents' house. Framed in narrow bands of dark teak, the monochromatic ink rendering of waves roiling against a rocky cliff was elegant in its simplicity. But the painting never belonged to us. *This is Mr. Yamamoto's painting*, my mother would remind my brothers and me. *If we ever find him we will give it back.*

And she would tell us the story about the day Mr. Yamomoto came to my grandparents' back door with the painting in his hands. The framed landscape had hung in the Yamamotos' home for twenty-five years. Mr. Yamamoto, an artist and a teacher, had painted it for his wife when their first child was born. But suddenly times had changed and the Yamamoto family no longer had the right to own property or live in their home on a quiet street in Oakland, California. The government of the United States had ordered them to report to a "relocation center" within forty-eight hours.

My grandmother took the painting and gave her word that she and her family would keep it for Mr. Yamamoto and his children. Each time she told the story, my mother would end it in the same way. *The Yamamotos lost everything because they looked like the enemy. They were sent to a re-location camp and we never heard from them again. What Americans did to the Yamamotos in the name of freedom was a terrible, terrible thing. It's up to you and me to never let anything like this ever happen again.*

My grandmother's promise to a neighbor and my mother's moral clarity are heirlooms I hold close in the surreal days since the world was turned upside down by a group of hate-filled men armed with pocket knives and box cutters. I find I am a member of an unpopular minority of Americans that calls for ordered justice rather than massive revenge and the re-evaluation of our uneven foreign policy. It is a lonely place to stand at a time when the world around me is wrapped in red white and blue and throbs with patriotic music and war drums. But I know it is where I belong. I think of the waves crashing against the rocks in Mr. Yamamoto's painting. And I remember my mother's words - *What America did ...in the name of freedom was a terrible, terrible thing. It's up to you and me to never let anything like this ever happen again.*

Little Hannalore

Anthony Garavente

It was the first time I was scheduled to teach on a Saturday morning, one of those U.S. History surveys that is a requirement for graduation. The class of twenty-five consisted mostly of those people the university referred to as "returning students," adults who had entered the work force or who had engaged in domestic chores after graduating from high school. Years of experience as a part-time lecturer—"adjunct faculty" in the officialese of university administrators, "freeway flyers" to those of us who have to teach on more than one campus to earn a living—had taught me that I couldn't lecture for the entire three hours each Saturday. The students would flee the premises during the mid-class break I needed or they'd show up after the intermission, and when you're hired from semester to semester as an academic serf in the feudal system that is modern academia, a half-empty classroom is not a recommendation for continued employment.

When I distributed the course syllabus promptly at nine o'clock that first morning, even before I checked the roll, there were some scowls and groans from the assembled students. One middle-aged woman ostentatiously rose from her seat nearest the door in the back of the room and muttered, "A quiz every week? Why, that's ridiculous!" Thereupon, she spun on her heels and made a hasty departure.

"Well, you can't please everybody!" I quipped, then launched into my prepared statement that a nine AM-to noon Saturday class could be an invitation to absenteeism and tardiness, which would undermine the quality of the course and jeopardize my position as its teacher.

"One of the reasons for the quizzes is to get you here each week on time. What kind of a class will it be if people wander in all through the morning?"

Before I could go on to another point in my procedural statement, a petite woman in a pink nurse's uniform piped up from the seat directly in front of me.

"What are the other reasons for the weekly quizzes?"

"They are meant to prevent procrastination on doing the weekly reading assignments," I responded quickly, grateful for the opportunity to state my case. "It's been my experience, when I only gave two midterms and a final exam for the course grade, that too many students postponed their reading until the night before the first midterm and ended up failing miserably, thus putting themselves in a deep hole."

To this information the petite nurse nodded vigorously.

"Also," I continued, encouraged by her receptivity to my teaching methods, "it spreads out the grade, which is better for the students."

"That sounds very sensible to me," she said and flashed a smile that caused the corners of her eyes to crinkle.

I smiled back at her, recognizing at once that I would have at least one attentive student in the class. That was how I was introduced to Hannalore Puppedorn, someone who, from the very first encounter, seemed to be young and old at the same time. Her short stature and slender figure, accentuated by neatly-cropped blonde hair, made her appear adolescent, but her face, despite the large pale blue eyes, and especially a guttural voice, revealed an older person. "Little Hannalore," as I began to refer to her in my mind, could have been a woman in her fifties. The "maturity" this tiny nurse exuded was helped along by an unfamiliar accent, which gave her words a softened German or Eastern European sound. By the third class meeting, while I was writing some information on the blackboard, I overheard her inform another student that she could speak Portuguese.

It was also at this time that the class had taken its second true-false quiz and was reminded of the first multiple-choice test it would take in the fifth week.

"Folks," I explained to the scattering of dirty looks that announcement evoked, "it's important to me that this class not be viewed as a Mickey Mouse course. I'm only a freeway flyer, not a secure, tenure-track regular!"

Little Hannalore chuckled, then politely asked, "What the goodness is a freeway flyer?"

"To make a living, I have to teach at more than one state university, as well as in two community colleges," I responded.

She shook her head in consternation at my harried teaching situation, to which I nodded my appreciation of her sympathy; thus, the good rapport we gradually developed with each other began on that very fist day. Little Hannalore was just the person I needed when I endeavored to elicit some class discussion, always a difficult undertaking with those students (alas, the majority!) who wanted only to be rid of what they saw as a troubling academic requirement.

Though a mere shadow of the Confucius of my Chinese history studies in graduate school, I did try to ask the kind of pointed questions worthy of the great sage, ones that would enable these poor captive students to lean on both the readings and the lectures, so it wouldn't be that difficult to take part in the discussion. I really wasn't asking for much!

"You don't want to sit there the entire three hours listening to me," I tried to cheer them on, knowing in my innermost heart that it was precisely what they preferred doing. "Let's hear from one another; it'll enrich the learning experience!" I said this with a straight face, hoping that it didn't sound too rah-rah.

But the boredom of the majority was often palpable, with some of them even seeming hostile. It was during low points like these when Little Hannalore would come to my aid with a sensible, if cautious, question or comment; though I had recognized early in the semester that she had no great interest in the study of history. For her it seemed to be a matter of doing well in the course.

"Class participation is fifteen percent of the final grade," she once cautioned the shy student sitting nearest to her. "That could be the difference between an A or a B."

But I didn't care what her motivations were. I had already noted that she was listed on the class roster as a health sciences major, probably taking classes to improve her employment prospects in that field. *A hard-working caregiver with no real interest in history is fine with me, I thought. The important thing is her participation, not what fuels it.*

When we were dealing with the Progressive Movement, nurse Puppedorn gave a fine biographical sketch of Margaret Sanger and spoke with authority about the history of birth control too, concluding her remarks by saying, "We could certainly use a dedicated person like Sanger on the birth control front today!" It was an inspired comment which came just short of arousing applause from me and from some of the other students who were tuned into that day's discussion.

She seemed hesitant, I did notice, in saying much about the First World War, except to nod vigorously to my view that the participation of the United States had more to do with economic ties to Great Britain than to Germany's unrestricted submarine warfare.

"After all," I reminded the class "the *Lusitania* was sunk in May 1915, almost two years before Wilson asked for a declaration of war on Germany."

"A very good point!" Little Hannalore commented to my interpretation.

When a Latino student asked about the importance of the Zimmermann Telegram as a "crude German effort" to provoke Mexico into declaring war on the United States in order to regain her territories lost in the Mexican-American War, Little Hannalore's hand shot in the air demanding my immediate attention.

"Wasn't the Zimmermann Telegram just a ruse by British intelligence, an example of what is nowadays called 'dirty tricks'"?

"Yes, there are some historians who have suggested foul play by the British," I responded cautiously, "but the timing of the U.S. declaration of war so soon after the March Revolution in Russia, I think, was a more decisive reason for Wilson's decision."

"Of course," Little Hannalore piped up, "the American president was worried about the Bolsheviks!"

"No Puppedorn," I corrected her, "the Bolshevik Revolution came in November. Wilson was worried that the March uprising would lead to Russia's withdrawal from the war."

After I lectured on a favorite topic of mine, the development of Jazz in the 1920s from Louis Armstrong to Duke Ellington, a subject that aroused more interest in the class than was usual, Little Hannalore approached me at the break, her doll-like face brightened by a big smile and asked, "Do you like *bossa nova*? "

"It's okay... I like it all right," I responded cautiously to her hopeful gesture for my approval of a style of jazz that she obviously admired. "I've always been a fan of Stan Getz."

"Yes, he plays the saxophone beautifully," she agreed, "but what of that kind of music?"

"Well," I prevaricated, needing a drink of water and the restroom, "swing and bop are much more to my liking."

"I grew up in Brazil," she said offhandedly.

I smiled at the *non sequitur*, then left the room.

When I talked about the causes and effects of the Great Depression that swept the United States after the stock market crash of October 1929, Little Hannalore was especially attentive from her usual seat right in front of my desk.

"And it was not only in America that it was felt," she commented when I paused to take questions. "The Great Depression was a worldwide disaster."

"Yes, that's quite true," I quickly agreed, "but this being a U.S. History course..."

"Didn't it actually begin in Europe?" she interrupted me. "My own parents always spoke of it as a momentous calamity that finished off the...European middleclass."

"Yes, the bank failures wiped out the savings of many who thought their future was secure," I answered her.

"What disillusionment that must have caused with ordinary people!" Little Hannalore exclaimed. "Their world was suddenly collapsing all around them."

I nodded decisively, not only to demonstrate my agreement with her assessment of this economic catastrophe, but also in appreciation of her stimulating the discussion which was joined by a few other students that day to make for a very successful class meeting. *"Many thanks, Little Hannalore!"* I muttered to myself when the session ended that morning and hurried to my car with a spring in my step.

Little Hannalore was proving to be so reliable a discussant that I didn't wait for her to raise a question but began calling on her when I was through lecturing in order to get the class discussion underway. During our evaluation of the New Deal she lucidly explained how the Agricultural Adjustment Act worked and gave a sympathetic presentation of Dr. Francis Townsend's scheme to bring relief to the aged poor during the Great Depression, linking it nicely with the passage of the Social Security Act in 1935.

"It really wasn't a bad idea!" she concluded with some passion in her voice.

I began the lecture on the Second World War with an account of the rise of Fascism in Italy, explaining how it germinated among those Italians, especially the veterans of the First World War, who were disillusioned by the Treaty of Versailles.

"Italian nationalists were chanting bitterly that their country had won the war but lost the peace," I said. "It was an emotional claim that was receptive to broad segments of the Italian population after the fighting in the trenches had ended, especially among the middleclass who feared economic ruin and radical revolution."

"Now the Bolshevik threat came into play?" Little Hannalore asked tentatively.

"Yes, that's right," I agreed. "The Bolshevik Revolution struck a responsive chord with Italian workers and there were active Socialist and Anarchist forces operating in the country by 1919."

I gradually began to view this tiny nurse almost like a teaching assistant, so helpful a member of the class did she prove to be. And she was always in her seat in front of my desk when I entered the room each Saturday morning, so that we got into the habit of nodding and smiling at each other before I actually got started. *If only I had a student like this one in all my classes throughout the long work week!* I lamented. *How much easier my teaching situation would be!*

As I moved deeper into the Second World War, I noticed that Little Hannalore was not her usual ebullient self. She preferred listening to what I had to say, staring intently at me in a way I hadn't perceived before.

"Fascism took such a strong hold in Italy in great part because it was seen by the Western democracies as a bulwark against Communism," I said. "Benito Mussolini, the flamboyant *duce* of the Italian people, was generally viewed favorably in the United States right up to the time Italy invaded Ethiopia in 1935."

"I heard he wasn't too popular," a black student commented, "among American blacks."

"Yes, that's quite true," I agreed, "but, except for leftwing and black publications, which had limited influence with the American majority, Mussolini had a fairly good press in the United States. *Colliers,* a magazine with a mass circulation, gave *il duce* space in its pages."

Little Hannalore sat quietly during these comments of mine, though completely absorbed in what I was saying.

"The brutal Italian subjection of Ethiopia and, more importantly, the rise of Adolf Hitler and the victory of Nazism in Germany, slowly changed American opinion," I continued, inadvertently casting a glance at Little Hannalore, whose expression had become anxious, almost grim, in that moment, a fact which should have alerted me to what was coming. "The Nazis practiced a particularly virulent form of Fascism, their national chauvinism crossing the line into a racism that was a direct cause of the Holocaust." I paused to survey the class, taking due note of Little Hannalore's silence and the blank stare that was now clouding her face. "Incredible as it may sound, the Nazis methodically exterminated, and that's the proper word for it, more than six million Jews, men, women and children, during their devastation of Europe."

"Well, of course it sounds incredible!" Little Hannalore interjected in a very self-assured manner. "There weren't that many Jews in the entire world at the time!"

Though I was blindsided by her skeptical comment and the cold contempt that echoed in her voice, I quickly regained my composure; however, I noticed the hand in which I already had a tremor had begun to shake.

"Oh, that's not true at all, Puppedorn! The figure of six million Jewish victims of the Nazi terror probably represents a minimum one, there being another two million never accounted for, people who disappeared."

She shifted in her seat at my sharp reaction, just the suggestion of a smile altering her blank expression, but it was that slight quiver in her chin that caused me to underscore my rebuttal.

"Remember, there were twelve million Holocaust victims; the Nazis considered other peoples besides the Jews as untermenschen. Their attitude that some of the races of Europe, Jews, Gypsies, Slavs were *subhuman* led them to initiate a particularly brutal military policy on the Eastern Front."

Though disappointed and even angered by this Holocaust denier, I couldn't forget that she was a student and I had been encouraging my students, especially this tiny nurse, to speak their minds freely. Discourage opinion and you discourage discussion was a guideline that I had always tried to follow. And while it was true that I had been disappointed by students before the revealing exchange with Little Hannalore, the thorn behind this rose was a long-pointed one.

"On the Eastern Front we...Germany faced the ruthless Communists," Little Hannalore protested, but in a carefully modulated voice, "the *situation* determined the...harshness of the fighting."

"No, I don't think that says it all," I quickly countered, aware by this time that I had the rest of the class to consider. "The Gypsies hunted down by the SS extermination squads in the forests of central Europe and the Jewish children who were gassed in the Nazi concentration camps were certainly not ruthless Communists!"

When I paused to clear my parched throat, my left hand shaking violently, she smiled patronizingly and asked, "Are you Jewish?"

Releasing a breath I wasn't even aware I had been holding, which miraculously stopped the tremor in my weak hand, I fixed her with the coldest stare I could conjure.

"No, Puppedorn, I'm not." I said in a clear voice that surprised me, considering the agitation in my breast. "I'm a historian; the facts of the Holocaust are well documented."

Though I felt I had "uttered the last word" in the tense exchange with the tiny nurse on this particular day, and that was important to my relationship to the other students, there was no joy in my heart when the class ended. I had a sour taste in my mouth and the beginning of a headache as I walked wearily to my car. *Did I handle the situation properly?* I berated myself silently. *Was the anger I experienced obvious to the class? After all, I've always had a "righteous" leftwing message I've been trying to get across, despite my efforts at objectivity. Can I complain, get angry, when I bang heads with somebody with a different point of view? I couldn't very well jump all over one of my students!*

I stood outside my old car fumbling for the keys, my fingers not working well, and noticed that it was a beautiful day and I didn't have to be back in the classroom until Monday morning. Then I sat behind the steering wheel longer than usual, the gnawing sensation of uncertainty pressing against my heart preventing me from starting the engine. *What the hell are we supposed to do with these freaking history surveys?* I sighed as I pumped the gas pedal to make sure the car started. "Freeway flyers got to have wheels," I muttered. "Don't you let me down!" When my faithful old vehicle turned over, I fairly shouted out the opened window, "Yeah, I'm out of here!" But as I exited the parking lot I had a last thought on the day's happenings. *That winsome little doll a damned Holocaust denier!*

All Will Abide

Maura Madigan

She clenches
her eyelids
as the first
stone flies.
It kisses
the top
of her right
ear and drops
lamely to
the ground barely
drawing dust.

Bearable, she
thinks, opening
her eyes, breathing
waiting for the
next and the
next until the
waiting is
over.

She flexes
her fingers
in the soft
earth, as it
hugs her body
packed tightly
against her limbs
her torso, only her
head visible
like a ripe cabbage
nestled in the garden.

Two more
rocks connect
with their
target and
she feels the
skin on
her forehead
open, warmth
like sweat drips
into her eye. She
longs to whisk
it away, but
she cannot and
this is when
her calm begins
to disintegrate.

The wind
picks up the
dust, throwing it
in her eyes, her nose
and suddenly she's
coughing, crying
searching the crowd
for help. Surely
someone will
stop this? Her mother, her
aunt, even her
sister whose jealousy
brought her here
to this spot
this fate. She
never thought
it would get
this far.

Just one kiss,
he said, *No*
one will know. No
one but Allah.

She knows
she can fight
this, claw
her way
out. It is written
and all will
abide, but she
did not think
it possible. No
one had.

Another rock, bigger
sharper, finds its mark
in one fierce
lick as she
bites her lip
to blot the
pain. She points
and flexes her
toes quickly, her hands
working in
unison, hidden. She
has not decided
if she wants
to fight
or surrender, the
latter easier
more honorable.

He was mine, her
sister had
yelled. *But you've
ruined it, just like
you've ruined
everything including
yourself.*

The rocks
come faster
now, pecking
groping, the faces
in the crowd
sweating with
exertion, the afternoon
sun in their
faces, blinding them
to the task.

Her arms
free themselves
soil like water
dripping from her
sleeves, a
rebirth. She claws
at the earth
around her waist
her legs, more
quickly now
impulsively
as the rocks
become bigger
faster more
vehement. Running
her tongue over
her teeth, she feels

jagged edges, blood
in her mouth and
knows that even
if she frees
herself, she can
never be
free.

Grief

Joel B. Peckham, Jr.

I've been thinking more and more about the nature of grief—what it is and how we respond to it. My father has been writing me about the sadness my mother has fallen into. She only recently lost her mother to cancer, and now she wakes up in the night crying and can't seem to focus during the days for lack of sleep. Though a trained counselor, my father struggles to find the words and actions that can help her. This is a hard read from so far away. I knew that my grandmother would almost certainly pass while I was out of the country on a Fulbright scholarship to Jordan, but there was nothing I could do to prevent my absence. I am thankful that my mother and father have each other and my sisters to hold each other up.

Still, I don't think we, as a culture, handle grief well at all—especially second-hand. Once, on a bus trip from Atlanta to Holland, Michigan, I had the opportunity to witness something astonishing. We were stopped over in Nashville at about 3am. The station was surprisingly full and active—though with the activity of sleepwalkers: exhausted travelers trying to unfold dollar-bills and stuff them into vending machines, trying to catch a few winks against a wall, trying to position themselves in the right place, near the doors, so when the bus was fueled and clean and ready, they could find choice places in line and choicer places on the busses, near the doors, against the windows, far from the stink of the toilet in the back. I was simply trying to shake off the weight of my own concerns when everything seemed to come alive in a burst of activity and shouting: "Mister are you alright?" "You need a doctor—somebody call an ambulance." There by the ticket counter a man had dropped to his knees, a few dollars spread out on the floor by one of his hands, an old leather pouch a few feet away.

My first thought was that he had had a heart attack and people were responding with appropriate, even effective concern. But soon it became apparent that his health wasn't the problem. He lifted his chin and we could see that he was weeping. When people began to realize that he was not dying, but "merely" suffering, they backed off—leaving about three feet all around him. They looked away, spoke in low whispers to each other. No one touched him, or approached him any longer, as if they feared that by entering his pain, it might become their own. Or maybe they were scared: "is he insane?" " Is he dangerous or contagious?" By appearances you wouldn't think so. Though not wealthy, he was well dressed, clean-shaven, old but not old to the point where you wondered if his mind had gone. Perhaps some were angry, felt duped, upset that their real concern for his health was misplaced. Eventually he got up and walked to the restroom, a bit wobbly but composed. I didn't see him again. But I think of him.

How many of us hold in our pain as if embarrassed by it? How many seem even more embarrassed at the sorrow of others. We don't know what to do with our hands. We don't know what to say. Since coming to the Middle East, I've felt the last vestiges of my New-England stoicism dropping away and I don't regret it. Here in Jordan emotions are hot and shared. Both joy and sorrow even sound the same, hard coughs coming up from the gut, like the sounds a frozen river begins to make in spring as the ice melts and booms. And it ends the same, in tears. Sometimes I wonder if the intensity of the Arabs isn't what makes so many Americans fearful of them. Beamed across oceans by satellite, images of Palestinians in Gaza or Iranians in Bam beating their heads with their hands in public grief and anger seem more than foreign to us; they approach our conceptions of insanity. Better to hold it in or become shell-shocked rather than end up on the floor of some bus-station with strangers surrounding you, whispering about your mental health. But we could learn a little bit, I think, from these people.

A genuine community requires engaged people willing to do the hard work of risking themselves a little by exposing themselves to the often messy world around them—to walk willingly and bare-headed into the elements. We need each other more than we are willing to accept. At a poignant moment in one message, my father wrote that my mother's sorrow "is my life and I embrace it." That embrace is not only the best we can hope for and from each other, it may be the only defense we have against despair.

Ibrahim's Story

Richard Newman

I always buy candles when I invite
someone for supper. They remind me of
Erev Shabbat dinners I used to have
in the years before there was a Jewish State
with the families of my Jewish friends. Rafat,
village of my birth, is gone. Now I live
in Bethlehem, in exile, and weave
carpets, and write songs, and watch, and wait.

Once, sitting among stones on this land
we all call home, an American guide
told a teen tour group from the States that trees
my ancient namesake planted moved the breeze
around them, *roots nourished by Jewish blood.*
Like yours, I thought, moving on, gun in hand.

Out of Line

From the First Weeks in New York, If My Grandfather Could Have Written a Postcard
Lyn Lifshin

if he had the words, the
language. If he could
spell. If he wasn't
selling pencils but knew
how to use them, make
the shapes for words
he doesn't know. If he
was not weighed down
with a pack that made
red marks on his shoulder,
rubbed the skin that
grew pale under layers
of wet wool, he might have
taken the brown wrapping
paper and tried to write
three lines in Russian
to a mother or aunt he
might never see again.
But instead, too tired to
wash hair smelling of
burning leaves he walked
thru, maybe he curled
in a blue quilt, all he had
of the cottage he left
that night running past
straw roofs on fire,
dreamt of those tall black
pines, but not how, not
yet 17, he will live in
a house he will own,
more grand than any he
saw in his old country

The Barn

Adnan Adam Onart

When he reemerged from the barn
he was carrying a rusty canister,
not luggage or a bag.
The passport you ask for
is my ancestor's labor
that fertilized the orchards, he said.
Not in Russian, but in Tatar this time,
with a softness defying the gun
directed at him.
Then he lifted the canister toward the sky,
murmuring an ablution prayer.
The flames were all over his clothes
before even his cigarette touched the ground.
The police officer moved forward
as if he were going to fire his weapon.
Then he turned around:
started his bike,
and disappeared in a dust cloud.

I was eleven at that second,
turned sixty a second later.

And it never went away:
The smell of that gasoline
showering the erect body of my father,
and the odor of his burned flesh,
ninety percent, as the coroner
at the Lenin Hospital said.

The Police Station
23 June 1978, Besh-Terek, Crimea

Adnan Adam Onart

There was nothing I could do,
Comrade Commissar.
As you had requested
I went to his house
and I said:
we have no choice
but to put you in prison again.
He became agitated first.
This is my ancestral land, he said,
I don't need a passport here.
This is a Soviet district, I replied
and you are an illegal alien here.
When he saw my pistol, he calmed down.
Maybe I should have shot him right there.
Let me change my clothes, he said.
Let me say good-bye to my family.
I thought these were reasonable requests.
He disappeared for a short while into his barn.
When he came back, he had
a gasoline can in his hand.
To tell you the truth, I thought
he was going to pour it on me.
I immediately started my motorcycle.
Tried to start, I should say.
O that lazy Ukranian mechanic.
Next week, next week,
he has been telling me for months.
When it comes to fixing
politburo cars...
In any case, I tried to start the bike again:
not even a click.

I grabbed my pistol.
But in the blink of an eye, the crazy Tatar
poured the gasoline on himself,
set himself on fire – I didn't see exactly how.
There was nothing I could do, Comrade Commissar.
He was yelling at me in his own language
something with *Allah* in it.
Luckily the motorcycle started right that moment
and you would not believe
he was running after me – yes in flames.
I called the coroner at the Lenin Hospital.
90% burns: even his wife could not recognize him.
Of course, I'll put everything in writing
in a detailed report, first thing in the morning.

Lenin Hospital
23 June 1978, Besh-Terek, Crimea
Adnan Adam Onart

Musa, my Musa,
spirit of my spirit,
life giver to my children,
the flame of our righteous fight!

Woman, interrupts the man in white,
can you positively identify the corpse?
The woman turns around,
looks the coroner in the eyes,
without a touch of hesitation.
Yes, she replies, *this is my Musa all right.*

How, asks the coroner astonished,
how can you tell?

She becomes silent for a moment,
then gets closer to the rusty,
metallic tray,
points to a tiny cloud of ashes
rising from a hole –
in what used to be three hours ago –
the chest of a human body.
His heart, she says,
can't you see, his heart still burning
for Crimea,
our stolen ancestral land.

Pathetic Tatar, murmurs the coroner,
pushes the drawer
back into the refrigerator,
closes the door,
verifies the latch
and quickly fills out the form:

CAUSE OF DEATH:
    COMBUSTION, SELF-INFLICTED
DEGREE OF BURNS:
    FOURTH DEGREE – 90%
IDENTIFICATION:
    NEGATIVE
NOTE:
    EVEN HIS WIFE COULD NOT RECOGNIZE THE DEAD.

The Lesson

Marin Sorescu

In school, when I'm called on,
I give a scatterbrained answer,
No matter what the question.

"How are you doing in history?"
My teacher asks me.
"Badly, very badly.
I've just concluded a lasting peace
With the Turks."

"Define the law of gravity."
"Wherever we may be,
On water or on land,
On terra firma or in the ether,
All things are required to fall
On our heads."

"What stage of civilization would you say
We've attained?"
"The age of uncarved stone,
Since the only carved stone
Ever found,
The heart,
Has been lost."

"Do you know how to draw a map of our best hopes?"
"Sure, with colored balloons.
Each strong gust of wind
Blows another balloon away."

From all this, it's pretty obvious
I'll have to repeat the year.
Serves me right.

translated by
Adam J. Sorkin and Lidia Vianu

Out of Line

Always Bearded

Marin Sorescu

We let our beard cover us
With its wisdom,
And we walk solemnly down the street,
Appearing invested with grave wisdom
That radiates from us into all
Things.

But beneath the grass that hides us,
We know
That the majority of the knots
On which we cracked our teeth and mind
Have eluded our unraveling...

Our virile beard alone
Yet clings to hope.
It grows down under the earth
Where, like a vine, it takes root
And once more returns above,
Bearing fruit in our children,
In an historic resistance.

translated by
Adam J. Sorkin and Lidia Vianu

Out of Line

The Meet

Marin Sorescu

In a room like any other room,
Constructed with a sturdy ceiling,
We compete in the high jump.

We know unequivocally
That no one can jump
Higher than the ceiling,
Were he God himself.
This is because of gravity
Which has constantly dragged us down
Since the moment of creation.

But we keep at it
With diabolical persistence.
We can't do otherwise.
We're cursed with the daemon of elevation,
As flying fish have
An itch for real wings.
Day and night we keep at it
Under our low ceiling.

The most limber among us,
Who have the best conditioned muscles, and the strongest,
Who most skillfully get the hang of
The physical laws of the high jump,
Also get the biggest bumps on the head.

translated by
Adam J. Sorkin and Lidia Vianu

Nose Print

Marin Sorescu

It happened to Ioniță, Burghiu's son.
They would place the paper in front of people, who
Would cross their arms, in order not to sign.
"Put your finger here!"
"We can't read. We don't know how." Women would thrust their
      hands
Into their bosom. Men would keep their hands behind them,
Holding one tightly in the other, or they crossed them on their chest.
They said they couldn't even put their finger on it, since they
      couldn't read,
They would be summoned in turn into a little room at the
      Provisional Committee
–That's what they called the Town Hall–
Everything was provisional. Except the land, which they would take
Once and for all. A bunch of worthless good-for-nothings,
      well-fed and florid,
Potbellied, coming from who knows where to tell you what's what.
In that little room, as soon as a peasant came in, scrawny, scared,
Unshaven, feigning sickness, he'd stiffen. Fix his eyes
Hard on the floor— he'd rather watch
The kerosene sink into that worn flooring than look at the sheet
Of paper, waiting on the table, already written out.
(Paper there was plenty of at the time, for the applications.
The paper crisis came later.)
And as he stood there, one of them from the commission would
      come to him
And smear the tip of his nose with India ink on a brush
While another of them pushed his head from behind.
"Come on, bend over here."
"But I can't sign myself! In my day, they didn't teach you
Letters."
But the other kept pushing his head lower and lower...

Until he pressed his nose against the application...
And that was the signature. In India ink, with the tip of his nose.
That's how Ioniță, Burghiu's son, found himself signed up.

Others waved their hands all around and defended themselves.
So how did they deal with these people?
They had soapsuds ready, mixed with salt, in a basin.
It was night, they always summoned them to the council at night.
If they wouldn't come on their own, they'd fetch them in Ciușe's cart,
The Ciușe from Gura Racului. Those horses had grown gaunt from carrying people
Up the hill from the valley.
At the hour of lamp lighting, they'd start gathering them in,
To tell them what's what.
"Hey, my good friends, why don't they work in the light of day
Like honest people? Why only in the night, like thieves!
I'm not going, not me!"   Petrică, Nete's son, announced.
But they would find him, catch him in the stable, under the barn,
In the pile of corn cobs–then they'd put him in this good fellow's cart
And haul him to the Town Hall.
"Here, this way," they'd order, when they saw him enter, covered
With straw, wood chips, his beard tangled.
And they pushed him inside the room next door.
"Will you sign? Did you explain it to your woman?"
"No, 'cause she's sick."
Then they'd send the bailiff out in the cart again. They'd also get her.
From the pigs, right in the sty, where she aimed to hide herself.
They would put it before them.
"Now, just when will you be able to?"
"Well, we'll have to talk to our children, too, 'cause it's their land."
They'd say maybe sometime later.
Their children were in Craiova, gone away to school.
"Oh, really, and when did you last have a bath?"

First they'd take Vitilina. One of them held her, the other washed
Her head with the soap and salt. And the suds, they'd get them in
 her eyes.
The woman screamed, flailed about with her hands.
Finally one of them smeared her nose with ink...
And the other of them stuck the paper on...
Then they'd also take him...
They'd even be laughing:
"Let's not make a mountain out of a molehill. By the time your
 children come back,
You'll have taken care of the whole business.
And the state will take care of them."
So that was the signature.
"Now you can go home. Oh well, sorry, the cart's left already.
You can walk as far as Racu... But who knows, if you hurry,
Maybe you'll catch up with it."
Nae's Ionica, when she got out of there, blinded by the salt,
Couldn't find her way, she was going uphill to Bisa,
In the gully. She smacked her head against tree after tree, spewing
 forth a torrent of curses.
"May this all turn to ashes! May this village fall to dust,
You blind bastards!
May you be buried on my land,
And may the earth sicken with you and vomit you out of your
 graves
On your fat thrones. May the water dig you up... and may it
 wash you away dead,
Scum of the earth!"
The same thing happened to Marin Fănache and to Gheorghe
 Roncea.
Him, they told they'd hang high from the oak tree.
The other Ioniță, Bita's Mitru's son, the same.
Everyone thought: How can I go on living if I give them all my
 land?
Well, the people were right, of course. They had sound minds.
Yet they still couldn't conceive of what would come to pass,

How they were to become servants on their own land.
So that's the way it was taken from them, on the basis of a nose
    print.
Petrică, Nete's son, even started to ask around
Whether nose prints were valid before the law.
What law, huh? You fool, someone said to him,
They make the law.
You enrolled in the collective farm with your nose, you're signed up
    all legal-like.
You're not going to see your land back. Even if you hadn't enrolled,
They'd have found a way to take it.

                        translated by
                        Adam J. Sorkin and Bogdan Ştefănescu

Marin Sorescu (19 February 1936 – 8 December 1996), Romania's Nobel Prize nominee the year of his untimely death, was his country's most widely celebrated and frequently translated contemporary writer, particularly well known throughout Europe. A dozen books of Sorescu's poetry and plays have appeared in English, mainly in U.K. and Ireland, and his translators have included fellow poets Seamus Heaney, W.D. Snodgrass, Michael Hamburger, Ted Hughes, and Paul Muldoon. He is the author of more than 20 collections of poetry, among them *Poems* (1965), *The Youth of Don Quixote* (1968), *Cough* (1970), *Fountains in the Sea* (1982), *Water of Life, Water of Death* (1987), *Poems Selected by Censorship* (1991), and *The Crossing* (1994). In 1994-95, Sorescu served as Romania's Minister of Culture. His deathbed volume, *The Bridge*, translated by Adam J. Sorkin and Lidia Vianu, was published by Bloodaxe Books in 2004. A career retrospective, *The Past Perfect of Flight*, is due out soon in Romania.

                    — Biographical note by Adam J. Sorkin

The Exile Season: Are We Living a *New McCarthyism* or Just the Same Old Thing?

Diana Anhalt

The closest my father ever came to explaining why we fled the Bronx to Mexico, when I was a child, was the day before he died. My sister, brother and I sat by his bedside. We sang. (It gave us something to do.) He had a brain tumor, and the nurse claimed he probably couldn't hear us, but we sang anyway: the old labor songs–*Joe Hill, John Henry* and *Sixteen Tons*–folk songs like *Frankie and Johnny*–and the old favorites. We were singing: "It's still the same old story, a fight for love and glory, a fight to do or die..."when he opened his eyes and in a loud, clear voice announced: "Did I ever tell you I met your mother at a YCL (Young Communist League) meeting?" Then he lapsed into a coma, never to speak again.

Following the terrorist attacks on September 11, 2001, and the subsequent restrictions on personal freedom, I started to remember my own past. We left the United States in 1950 just as the anti-Red campaigns attributed to Joseph McCarthy and others were gaining ground. Mexico's liberal migration policies offered us, and others like us, some small rescue.

From one day to the next, I found myself in a country whose name I couldn't pronounce–I had lost my front teeth shortly before we left New York–whose language I couldn't speak, and whose water I couldn't drink. (At the beginning, that was the only good part. For months, ginger ale, forbidden me back home, was the only liquid that crossed my lips.)

Today, I can't help wondering whether the current outbreak of bigotry, directed in this case, against those of Middle Eastern extraction, is merely a cyclical phenomenon, like a flu epidemic. Are we doomed to periodic repetition? It's easy to believe we are, because once again, we are witnessing the curtailment of individual liberties.

Thus, I for one, imagine there must be Arab-American families out there as terrified as my parents must have been some fifty years earlier. In the wake of the tragedy, they too fear they might be swept up in the overzealous security measures being taken to "protect the nation." Perhaps, they are seriously weighing the possibility of leaving the United States–of walking away from their lives and migrating. Will they choose Mexico?

If they do, I can state with some authority, they could do a good deal worse. While migration may have been easier in the '50s than it is today, American citizens can still cross the border on a tourist card. However, legalizing their status in Mexico and finding some way to earn a living would doubtlessly be even more difficult for them than it was for us. The population has increased considerably, the quality of life has degenerated, suspicion of foreigners is on the rise, starting up a new business requires far more capital, and the cost of living is much greater than it was in our day.

Throughout the '50s, the FBI, which referred to us as the ACGM, (American Communist Group in Mexico), kept track of our movements, intercepted our phones, and fed misinformation to the press and potential employers. But, for the most part, we were able to pursue normal lives. True, we were occasionally arrested, deported, and denied residence papers, either with the full cooperation of the Mexican Government or without, but, for the most part, the political expatriates were able to operate businesses or obtain jobs, place their children in schools, pursue their interests and travel within the country.

Those are the kinds of things I could tell my hypothetical Arab-American families about, but there is a good deal I couldn't, because no one thought to tell me. One day we were in the Bronx. The next day we were in Mexico. My parents would remain in that country for the next thirty years. (I still live there.) On the few occasions when I screwed up my courage to ask why we had left home, my parents either feigned deafness, changed the subject, or left the room.

I would later learn we were among dozens of families who chose to leave the United States for Mexico because it offered a refuge for people who were dodging subpoenas–a number had been indicted for espionage–or who were blacklisted, targeted for deportation, fed up with the Red-baiting, or were convinced it was only a matter of time before the country would be taken over by Fascists.

Curiously, there are strong similarities between the two periods: Today we call it the *War Against Terror*. In those days we called it *The Cold War*. But both were battles waged against ideologies and fueled by fear–communism, on one hand, an extreme Muslim fundamentalism on the other. In both cases, it is hard to target the enemy– although the Cold War was directed against the Soviet Union, its satellites and the communist movement, in general. Today, though we target Afghanistan, Iran, Pakistan and religious fundamentalists affiliated with Islam, the enemy seems far more diffused than in the past. Though warfare has changed drastically in the ensuing decades, the tools employed to control dissent are surprisingly similar.

Within days of the September 11 attack, an anti-terrorist bill, entitled the *Uniting and Strengthening America by Providing Appropriate Tools Required to Intercept and Obstruct Terrorism Act* was rapidly pushed through the U.S. Congress. While the government has offered some persuasive arguments in defense of such drastic measures, one worries about abandoning those very principles that, one would like to believe, help distinguish us from the tyrants. It allows for unconstitutional searches, secret trials, ethnic profiling, and suspension of due process. This bill also punishes individuals for vague associations with possible terrorists.

Some of the same types of restrictions had been in place during the '50s. However, many others–not in present use–were institutionalized. Between 1947 and 1954 a series of anti-subversion statutes and practices, later declared unconstitutional, would give the government space to maneuver in. The FBI compiled the Security Index identifying those to be detained and sent to camps in the event of a national emergency. Loyalty Boards, unhampered by due process, screened thousands of federal employees. In addition, job seekers and passport applicants were required to sign loyalty oaths. The State Department routinely denied passports, the FBI tapped phones, employers scrutinized blacklists before filling a position, and paid informers crisscrossed the country. Most vulnerable were those U.S. resident aliens suspected of left-wing sentiments. They could be deported.

The curtailment of individual liberties–both then and now–was intended to combat the elusive enemy but, ironically, may have proved counterproductive: It resulted in sealing borders, tightening immigration restrictions and reducing travel.

Such isolationist tendencies are troubling, more so today than in the '50s, when "globalization" was little more than a theory and people were more likely to stay put. Nowadays, all that has changed, and the only way the U.S. administration can effectively stem terrorism is through the formation of an international coalition. In today's world, mainstream thinking is beginning to embrace such concepts as "diversification," "global village," "political correctness," and "NGO."

Thus, while isolationism ceases to be a goal, or even a possibility, the movement to impose internationally accepted standards of justice and humane treatment is strengthened. Moral indignation at human rights abuse and the impunity of dictators is widespread. Access to information and the ability to command an audience is fomenting change and will, most likely, continue to do so.

If I am right–and I sincerely hope I am–those Arab-American families fearing persecution will not have to follow in my parents' footsteps. They will not have to flee the United States nor reside for decades, as my parents did, in a foreign country.

In 1980, at the height of the Reagan era, my father and mother returned to the United States. They were no longer the middle-aged couple that had arrived with young children and $1000 dollars in life savings. By then, they had acquired a taste for highly seasoned food, unrestrained color, and mariachi music sung slightly off-key. In addition, they would carry with them an undying gratitude, respect and affection for Mexico and the Mexican people who took them in–no questions asked.

I would like to believe, given the advances that have taken place over the past fifty years, that nowadays human rights in the United States will never be abused to the extent they were in the '50s. After all, I keep telling myself, *Bushism* really doesn't have the same ring to it that the word *McCarthyism* does.

Out of Line

NATURAL AND HUMAN WORLDS

V

On Earth Day 2003

Joanne Seltzer

I share the metal awning
of my home
with drab sparrows
who clogged the drainpipe
twice last year,
brought two new broods
into this crowded world.

They gather dry grass—
perhaps they dream
life will continue
until the sun burns up
a million years from now
as if nukes did not
proliferate
or global warming grow
the ozone hole
or acid rain split genes.

When the rain stops
sunshine will slowly
bleach my blue sofa
and the cat will bask
in her bow window
paws up like a lion
and the birds will sing.

Uses for Gypsum
Calcium Sulfate

Sharon Carter

Perhaps you already know your wall board
and underlay were once mined in Utah
or our cereal and sliced bread

are fortified with *Snow White Calcium,*
that it makes excellent pottery molds
as well as the finials on our state buildings.

Perhaps you have read it is cheap filler
for pharmaceuticals, that there is a namesake
town in Colorado, where, in 1905,

Teddy Roosevelt's hunting party killed
ten bears and two bobcats.
Maybe you knew human bones

are mostly calcium phosphate,
but not that forensic experts in Iraq
rely on gypsum's glistening footprint

to identify mass graves. This alone
provides two hundred and seventy
reasons for its usefulness.

SNOW DROPS

Gemette Reid

I
hear
snow drops
fall
twisting green caps
within
war's clamor,
media's warped claims
unknown pain,
families running from tanks,
torn apart by greed
will they see
my snow drops
praying
for peace, as pure spirits
remember beauty?
inner serenity
turned upside down
slanting green
stalks
matching caps
spreading over rough
lawn,
while war disappoints
everyone
from Thucydides
on?

Spring Trumps World News, May 2003

Maureen Tolman Flannery

I left the house preparing to mind-write a ranting diatribe
about what this wielding a fist against the world
has done to the things I value most,
not the least of which is the meaning of words.
I was geared up for indignant lashing out
at officialese, its inaccurate naming of things,
how words are conscripted from their simple working lives
and ordered against their will to show up
in such phrases as *friendly fire,* or *smart bombs.*
But before I had turned the first corner
a patch of jocular pansies out-danced
the aftermath of war in its bid for attention.
Magnolias exploded into pink
down streets that just weeks ago
showed only sleet and bare-gray scaffolding of trees.
Now whole blocks present blossoming pear trees
all clean and airy like a pew of first communion girls
veiled to wed the consecrated host,
like scallops of wedding lace on the train of a giant bride.
And isn't this world a bride again, all virginal and rosy
and waited upon by handmaidens that enhance her beauty.

Streamers of forsythia lean with the weight of yellow.
Color everywhere asserts itself like people too long pressed down.
Rhododendrons cascade mauve onto lawns' new green.
Rows of red uniformed tulips stand at attention
like a brass band ready to step off into a Sousa march.
Sky is ablaze with the huge flowering crabs
that burst overnight into vibrant rose.
Vitality that remains in this ground out-shouts politics.
My mind wanders from the plight of "enemy combatants"
to the simple hope that they can see such trees.

Morning Briefings

Bette Lynch Husted

All right, let's get this straight. Say Coalition
Forces. Death Squads, not The Fedayeen.
Liberation. Never use 'invasion.'
Speak with one voice. Just there: a winter wren
singing his small, whole-bodied celebration
amid bright moss, and something—ghosts of salmon?
crisscrossing April current, Soapstone Creek.
I tell you, boys, this isn't for the meek,

this job. Remember that you're representing God.
Tanks or air strikes–either way, we win.
This morning, three elk walking up the creek bed
like silent smoke out of the mist. Not one
afraid, or hurried. Quietly, they lead
each other up the trail. Vermilion
elderberries in July now just white
petaled clusters opening to light.

Red fox track in wet sand–in the elks' wake
bleeding hearts, pink-blazing shooting stars.
Regret the losses. But make no mistake:
We will not tolerate this threat of War
by Terror. Four mergansers rise, a quake
of russet, wingtips riffling the far
side of the pool. The hummingbird's returned
where last year something flame-red hung, and burned

Lessons

Mario Milosevic

No one told me I should not kill
but that first beetle I stepped on

had more power than any law.
It was the crackle of its hide

as I made it collapse on itself,
and the unexpected bulk of it,

the little life pushing against
my sole to the end and beyond.

Breaking those tiny fissures open
and the oozing there. Those faintly

thumping legs quivering long after
they should have stopped—had to

stop—for the horror of my power
to dissipate into something bearable.

And later, walking past the place
seeing the stain even weeks after

the event, and hearing the death
rattling in my head, those scraping

legs swimming in air, the will of
them saying it was not ok to take.

Annual Pigeon Shoot, Higgens, PA.

Marian Kaplun Shapiro

This morning, Labor Day, the news
at seven finds me half-listening,
waiting for the promised
Habanera of Bizet, and later
for a new orchestral Gaite'
Parisienne. A bomb has caused
"collateral damage" somewhere
in the Middle East (that means
that children have been killed).
Florida warns its residents:
the con men are slithering
in the wake of the looters
across the path of rubble
of the first Fall hurricane. *Of course.*
What else? Soon Bizet. Then Offenbach.
But one more item before
The weather for Boston and vicinity
(will it warm up enough
to have the usual barbecue?)
From Higgens, Pennsylvania, we learn,
the annual pigeon shoot is underway.
(People shooting pigeons? Well, perhaps
they are a plague, a Tienneman Square
of raucous birds, carriers of disease...)
The newscaster continues: The way
it's done, he says, is fixed by ritual.
Crammed into crates, the birds
are starved. Thus, a very few
can fly when freed. Those get away.
The others are shot down. Presumably,
it doesn't take too long. Plenty
of time to picnic. Probably

the winner gets a prize. This year
there are a few protestors,
bussed in from New York.
The mayor is annoyed. New York, of all
places! People should learn
to tend to their own back yards!
Mind their own business, and leave
each to his own.

Radio News

Susanna Lang

The newscast says they're overrun with skunks
out west. It hasn't rained, the ground's packed hard.
No insects shimmer in the afternoon.
The skunks will share the bowl you left to feed
your dog, they'll hunt for slugs inside your compost,
dig for grubs in lawns you've stolen water
to keep green. You call, you've got a skunk,
you want the cops to come.
                      Arrest a skunk.

The interviewer asks the deputy,
How do you avoid a scent release?
The answer is, you don't. I want to ask,
*And what do you prefer, the stink of fear
or just a glimpse of stripes, a wedge-shaped head
among the melon rinds and coffee grounds?*

FULL CIRCLE

Susan H. Case

Begin in desert; end with
splat of real estate.
Low-built flat-roof add-ons
hitched to fast-assembly
Lego dreams:

Circle K
strip mall
billboard
golf clinic
unkempt sand.

When certain ridges
in the Rincons slope
just right, I could twirl among them
full circle, pretend
there is no sprawl out there.

The trail I picture with my eyes closed
promises to angle down through arroyos
that should be laced with Gila Monsters
flashing jewels of beaded orange.

But here, fake stucco
brick face,
cinderblock
crawl toward where I stand.

Almost always
the expensive view remains unseen.

Prairie Storms

Fredrick Zydek

Out on the plains we hear these storms
coming long before they get here.
They rumble like spirits of buffalo herds
stampeding their way back into history.

I shrink into my shadow and wait
for what I know the wind will do
once it's fully awake, beating its enormous
drums and lighting the terrible fires that will

live in the air, light that is more than light,
rage that is more than rage, a luminary
crack of combustion that snaps through air
like pain down the spine. I grow thin

at the edges, remember that in the end
I'm helpless as the birds who have taken
shelter in the trees. I want to be a mole
burrowing deep beneath the elms, safe as dirt.

Soon the sun slips, swollen and nude
into the wind's nasal questions. Consume
me wind! Fill my bones with what the seasons
fear but will not tell. I think I know whose names

are bellowed from the belly of these storms.
They are primordial, older than DNA, want me
to understand that no matter what,
my skin will never be enough to save me.

Visiting the Niagara

Fredrick Zydek

This water means business.
It's a place where
the planet's urge to wash
all things out to sea
grows almost out of control.

Everyone knows that water
can bellow and roar, but who
would have guessed it could
sing. We must find new ways
to salute this holy place.

This is nature's way
of reminding us our imaginations
will never be enough.
What happens here brings awe
even to those who hibernate

in archaic and dismal gods.
These waters know things
not even clouds are allowed
to tell. Stones here know
as much about being wet

as any rock secreted by the sea.
Even the air is different
here. This may be the only
place on terra firma where rain
is less than half the matter.

CREATING A BETTER WORLD

VI

Post-9/11: Trauma, Nonviolence and Self-Protection

Steven Morr-Wineman

The events of September 11, 2001 have placed trauma on the center stage of world politics. In the aftermath of the attacks against the World Trade Center and the Pentagon, massive numbers of people experienced a bone-deep sense of violation, helplessness, powerlessness, terror, and rage. These are core phenomena associated with trauma. In turn, this mass experience of victimization has been mobilized politically in the service of counter-aggression, war, and a frontal assault on civil liberties.

The sense of victimization and subjective powerlessness that so many Americans understandably feel in the wake of September 11 stands in stark contrast to the overwhelming dominance that the U.S. actually wields globally in the economic, political, and military spheres. Objectively, the U.S. remains the world's sole superpower. The terrorist attacks, far from undermining that position, have provided a pretext for the further consolidation and exercise of power. "Nothing more dangerous," Ariel Dorfman writes, "[than] a giant who is afraid."[1] It's not that most people are now unaware of the United States' position as sole superpower; it's that many people don't *feel* that power – and, even more to the point, don't feel sufficiently protected by the country's power.

I think that what a large number of people *feel* is that any day there could be a new terrorist attack, coming in any number of forms (biological, chemical, nuclear, and so on), that it could happen anywhere, and that they or their loved ones could be killed without warning and without any means of defense. That kind of sense of being acted upon, and the levels of terror and rage that it evokes, simply drown out the relevance or significance of American dominance for many people. In turn, the intolerable sense of subjective powerlessness that underlies traumatic terror and rage creates an exceedingly fertile base for popular support of counter-aggression that can be defined as self-protection and self-defense.

We are at a moment when we urgently need alternative understandings of how to protect ourselves against attack. We need a concept of self-protection rooted in an awareness of how violence *crushes the human spirit* of those who enact it, whether we enact violence from the stance of perpetrator or from the stance of victim. This essay explores ways that we can use nonviolence as a method of self-protection – not simply as a political theory or ethical framework (though it surely is both), but also as a vital practice, coming from the heart as well as the head, which can effectively break cycles of violence.

Nonviolence From the Head and From the Heart

Commitment to nonviolence is something I feel in my bones. When I learned of the terrorist attacks on 9/11, my first reaction was stunned horror. My next reaction was to be terrified of what the U.S. government would do in response – of the cascade of violence that this event could unleash. And my next reaction, which I remember saying out loud, was that the only sane response to the horror of those attacks was nonviolence. That the only way to reduce violence in the world is to practice nonviolence.

I know that last line sounds like a political slogan. And it's true that it came out of many years of political thought and action, out of my own identification with nonviolent politics. But the point is that it was a gut reaction, a felt response – a heart response as well as a head response.

At a very different level of politics, I don't hit my child because I feel so deeply that it would be wrong. It is the *depth* of my values that makes hitting or any kind of physical attack not an option for me, no matter how desperate and out of control, how victimized and powerless I feel – and I have felt all of these things as a parent a lot more often than I wish were the case. My commitment to nonviolent parenting, which certainly is something I have thought out and analyzed at great length, *lives* in my body.

I could say that when I don't hit my kid in moments of rage, it's an act of love, and it would be true. But there are many, many parents who love their kids as much as I do – and who hit their kids. Nonviolence shapes the way I'm able to use my love for my child. It gives me a very tangible resource for containing my most destructive potentials as a parent, in the moments when I am most at risk from the lethal combination of *feeling* powerless and when I am *acting* from a position of objective dominance.

What I am trying to describe is an *impassioned* commitment to nonviolence. Something that includes rational analysis, but that also pierces the surface of ideas to the depths of how we define ourselves and how we want to be in the world. I think it takes something at this kind of depth to counteract or re-shape the enormous force of traumatic rage.

At the level of personal identity, nonviolent resistance allows us to channel our rage into an impassioned determination *not to act like the people who have hurt and oppressed and traumatized us, and not to let our oppressors turn us into destructive people, even in the ways that we struggle against them or in our attitudes toward our perpetrators.* Aurora Levins Morales offers a moving example of the effective use of this kind of non-cooperation to maintain personal and political integrity in the face of torture:

> As a child...[f]or a period of several years, without the knowledge of my parents, I was periodically abused by a small group of adults who practiced physical, psychological, and sexual tortures, mostly, though not exclusively, on children. It was clear that their treatment of me had several goals. They deliberately confused and intimidated me so I would not reveal what was happening, but they also were attempting to reproduce themselves in me and the other children, to separate us from our own humanity enough to turn us into torturers as well.
>
> Because I was already a highly politicized child by the time

they got hold of me, because I already knew about political torture and resistance to it, I was able to develop a strategy that defeated them. They managed to keep me from telling, but I did not continue the cycle of abuse. I figured out that I was powerless to prevent what they did to my body but that I could safeguard my spirit. I understood that the first step in becoming like them was to learn to dehumanize others and that part of the goal of their cruelty was to make us hate them, make us want to hurt them, make us see them as monsters we would be willing to torment. To plant in us the seeds of their own pain.

Part of the way I prevented this was to envision my abusers as young children, before they became this cruel. I would imagine that imprisoned within the adult bodies that hurt me were captive children who had themselves been tortured. I would pretend that I could catch their eyes, send them signals of solidarity to give them courage. Imagine how horrified they were at the actions of their grown-up selves. This was what enabled me to survive spiritually.[2]

Levins Morales, a "highly politicized child," was clearly using her ability to analyze her situation and apply her political values to her struggle for self-protection. But her understanding enabled her to act from the place of her deepest humanity. Knowing that she could not protect her body, her struggle was for her spirit. Knowing that dehumanization destroys the human spirit, she developed an impassioned determination to connect with the mangled humanity of her torturers – enabling her to break a cycle of violence. This stands as an extraordinary expression of nonviolence coming from the head and from the heart.

At the level of movement politics, I think we saw that same quality of impassioned commitment to nonviolence in the civil rights movement. Nonviolence was a critical part of the civil rights movement's strategy. But it was also part of the movement's spiritual bedrock. This is particularly significant if we are willing to recognize that African-Americans were massively traumatized by Jim Crow practices in the South and by the entire legacy of slavery.

The civil rights movement achieved extraordinary success in mobilizing traumatized people to act constructively in the face of terror and rage. I think that this is largely attributable to the power of nonviolence as a response to trauma – not only as a principle, but as a living and breathing practice that people feel is connected to their own integrity as human beings.

In my view, nothing short of a radical re-emergence of this kind of nonviolent politics can stem the cycles of terror and counter-terror that have been unloosed in the world.

Nonviolence as Self-Protection

Aurora Levins Morales, as a child in the hands of torturers, knew that though she could not protect her body, she could protect her spirit. I take this to mean that she could take active measures to protect her human integrity, what was most essential and important about her as a human being. Her strategy for self-protection was to actively exercise nonviolence – to recognize, to fully respect and value the human core of her torturers. This was a conscious act of resistance. Levins Morales understood that her torturers wanted not only to attack her body, but also to crush her capacity for human connection. She fought them, and fought for herself, by staying connected to her own humanity and to theirs.

Self-protection is the precise spot where the politics of trauma and the politics of nonviolence intersect. The experience of abuse, violation, and traumatic powerlessness inevitably raises a core and enduring question in the lives of trauma survivors: how can we act effectively to protect ourselves? All too often, in the throes of traumatic reenactment and subjective powerlessness, we believe the answer is that we can't. As chronic victims, the ability to act effectively on our own behalf is what we most deeply want and need, and yet our subjective experience is that it remains beyond our grasp. Our need for self-protection, fueled by rage and distorted by traumatic powerlessness, too often is expressed in a desperate lashing that can do a great deal of damage at a personal level, and which at the level of mass politics can all too easily be manipulated into popular support for war and dehumanization.

Violence is readily understood as a means of self-defense, and it is undeniably true that physical violence is one way of trying to protect ourselves from physical attack. Because we live in a society that legitimizes many forms of violence in many contexts, the seemingly straightforward notion of using physical violence in self-defense merges seamlessly with the use of verbal violence in self-defense, with the "pre-emptive" use of violence, with acts of retaliation and revenge, with many types of aggressive and predatory behavior, and with all forms of dehumanization and oppression.

Wherever we find violence, we find people subjectively trying to protect and defend themselves. This runs the gamut from parents hitting kids to expressions of racism and homophobia, from male batterers who experience themselves as victims to justifications for U.S. aggression in the name of protection against terrorists. It is impossible to overstate people's fear of the Other, the need for self-protection evoked by that fear, and the damage caused by the legitimization of violence as a means of self-protection.

What's less obvious is the damage caused to ourselves by acts of violence. I am using violence in the broadest sense of acts and attitudes that treat people as Other, that dehumanize, that reduce people to objects, and that fail to recognize and affirm the core human value of the Other. In the process of treating others as less than human, we violate something essential about our own humanity. Thich Nhat Hanh writes that "[d]oing violence to others is doing violence to yourself."[3] This is exactly what Aurora Levins Morales realized in the hands of her torturers: that her human integrity was at risk from the impulse to dehumanize those who were dehumanizing her.

Even at the level of self-defense against physical attack, violence is a precarious strategy at best. If the attacker is physically bigger, stronger, and more aggressive, which is often the case, violent self-defense is likely to fail. Even worse, violent responses often evoke escalating violence from the attacker, placing the victim at greater risk. What passes for self-defense is often an impulse for retaliation in the aftermath of an attack, rather than an action that could actually ward off the attack and protect the victim.

In many cases nonviolent measures are more likely to protect the victim physically. These range all the way from fleeing or hiding to calling for help to talking calmly to the assailant to the use of nonviolent physical self-defense techniques that aim to stop an attack without hurting the assailant. Once I was approached menacingly by a man who, holding a lit cigarette, came up very close to me and asked me if I fight. We were in a narrow hallway, and I could not possibly have gotten away from him. I answered, simply and honestly, that I did not fight. He looked baffled and said, incredulously, "You don't fight?" I again told him that I didn't. He regarded me, hesitated, then turned and walked out the door.

In many other circumstances, no self-defense strategy will stop an attack. It may happen so abruptly and be over so fast that there is no time to respond in self-defense. (If the man who approached me had put the lit cigarette onto my face or punched me, rather than trying to intimidate me verbally, I would have been defenseless.) The imbalance of physical strength and force may be so overwhelming that physical self-protection is simply impossible, as is particularly the case when adults abuse children. The perpetrator may use means of violence – a gun, a bomb, an airplane crashing into a building – against which there is no feasible physical defense.

This is particularly important because most violence committed in the name of self-defense actually happens after the fact of the attack to which we are responding. This may be a matter of seconds: Someone tells me, "Fuck you"; I say "Fuck you" back. I may think that I'm responding in self-defense, and I may honestly be trying to protect myself. But what I'm really doing is counter-attacking. By the time I respond, the verbal attack against me is done. No amount of violence on my part, verbal or physical, will undo it. I may believe that by saying "Fuck you" back I'm protecting myself against a further attack. In fact I'm much more likely to be provoking a further attack.

The gap between the moment of attack and the use of violent self-defense is often much longer. Examples range from acts of personal retaliation or revenge to the state's use of the death penalty; from the cycles of terrorist attacks and counter-attacks by

Palestinians and the Israeli government to acts of war by the U.S. in response to 9/11. When violence is used in the name of self-defense after the fact, its object may or may not be the original perpetrator. The longer the gap between the original attack and the violent response, the more likely that the violence is being displaced onto someone other than the original perpetrator – with examples ranging from a child who evokes your own childhood trauma to the spurious linking of Iraq to 9/11.

In all cases when violence is used as a strategy for self-protection after an attack is an accomplished fact, it cannot possibly succeed in protecting the victim from an attack that has already happened. This seems so obvious that it would not need to be said – except that so many of us are driven so relentlessly to try to defend ourselves against the violations we have experienced in our pasts.

This is critically related to the dynamics of unresolved trauma. One of the key lessons from the study of trauma is that the effects of traumatic powerlessness long outlive their causes. Internalized powerlessness is a living reality for many trauma survivors. Subjectively, the moments of trauma are *not* simply "violations we have experienced in the past" – we experience them as an on-going reality in the present. This makes the use of violence to try to defend ourselves against traumatic powerlessness understandable. But it does not make it functional or effective.

If we are willing to expand the question of self-protection to include personal integrity – the safeguarding of human spirit and our capacity for human connection – the futility of violence becomes blatant. The more we dehumanize the other in the name of self-defense, the more we diminish our own humanity.

Even in the moment of attack, the question of how as victims we can protect our humanity is vitally important – not in place of, but in addition to the question of how we can best protect ourselves physically. But in the aftermath of attack, the challenge of self-protection shifts decisively to the area of personal integrity, of wholeness of spirit and the humanization of our experience. Whatever has been done to us physically cannot be undone. Counter-attack (verbal or physical) is likely to make us more vulnerable to future attacks. What we *can* do, in conscious resistance to our abuse, it to take active steps to treat others – both perpetrators and those who might become the displaced objects of our rage at our perpetrators – as full human beings. By doing that we actively and effectively protect our own humanity.

This is the realm in which nonviolent resistance is extraordinarily relevant to the situation of trauma survivors. In most cases the lasting, major damage caused by abuse is not physical but emotional and psychological – the crushing of human spirit. Efforts at self-protection by trauma survivors that demonize or dehumanize the Other – through physical violence, verbal violence, or other acts and attitudes that diminish the human value of those we experience as threats – unwittingly and tragically compound the damage to our own spirits. A central challenge faced by trauma survivors is how to resist malevolence and violation by valuing rather than diminishing human life.

Nonviolence redefines the terms of self-protection. It poses an entirely new set of questions: How can I safeguard my human spirit? How can I try to defend and protect myself physically without compromising or crushing my own humanity? How can I resist acts of abuse and oppression without dehumanizing my oppressors? How can I maintain human connectedness in the face of overwhelming malevolence? How can I take in and let myself feel the pain of what has been done to me rather than evading or numbing that pain through an act of violence? How can I take in the almost intolerably complex truth that I have been abused, demeaned, and disregarded by valuable human beings?

The strategy for self-protection that these questions point us toward is as relevant to mass politics as it is to personal recovery from trauma. For example, imagine a collective response to September 11 along the lines of Aurora Levins Moralesí response to her torturers:

We understood that there was nothing we could do to prevent the mass destruction caused by attacks that had already taken place. But we figured out a way to safeguard our collective human spirit. We tried to envision and let ourselves feel the human suffering that could lead people to become terrorists and could allow them to destroy human life on such a massive scale. We particularly understood how much they were diminished by not valuing the humanity of the people they destroyed. We committed ourselves to not letting the attacks diminish or destroy our own capacities to value human lives as broadly and as deeply as possible. We understood that this was how we could defeat terrorism.

The ability to actually use nonviolence as a means of self-protection – either personally or at the level of mass politics – is a matter of struggle. I write this as someone who has done my share of diminishing the human value of the Other over the years. The very forces of trauma that make nonviolence such a compelling strategy for self-defense are constantly moving us in the direction of violence. Dissociation, traumatic reenactment, terror, and unyielding subjective powerlessness are the crushing of human spirit and lead directly and incessantly to demonization and dehumanization in the name of self-protection.

Simply saying that nonviolence protects us better does not make it so. Nonviolence is something we need to learn to open our hearts to, and that is a long and hard-fought personal journey, and one that above all requires the willingness and the capacity to open ourselves to our own pain and to the pain of others.

For nonviolence to become a living and breathing reality – something that comes from the heart as well as from the head – also requires cultural, social, and political support. One of the reasons that the civil rights movement was able to mobilize the traumatic rage of African-Americans so effectively in the service of constructive social action was that the movement made the values of nonviolence so visible and prominent as a political force. It created a public context, something that people could readily grasp and take hold of.

I believe that we need to rebuild that kind of visibility and political articulation of nonviolence as a force for both personal and political change. September 11, both despite and because of its horror, has created an opportunity for a new dialogue about breaking cycles of violence. How to protect ourselves from violence is a conscious, urgent question for virtually everyone. The more we are willing to publicly discuss and explore nonviolence as a resource for self-protection, the more possible it becomes for people to entertain it as a value system, as a guide to actual behavior, and *as a way of coping with traumatic rage.*

Notes

1. Ariel Dorfman, "Letter To America," *The Nation* 275:10 (9/30/02), p. 22.
2. Aurora Levins Morales, *Medicine Stories: History, Culture and the Politics of Integrity* (Cambridge, MA: South End Press, 1998), pp. 111-112.
3. Thich Nhat Hanh, *Anger: Wisdom for Cooling the Flames* (New York: Riverhead Books, 2001), p. 70.

Shit Work

Sarah Littlecrow-Russell

In a dream I am helping an old warrior
Walk into the woods to die
Peacefully as a gnarled brown leaf
Settling at the base of an old Maple.
As we walk, I can feel death begin
To wrap his frail body in its red blanket.

Then he tells me he needs to shit.

I kneel down and push my hands
Into the softness of earth
Nails scraping like badger claws
As I dig a shallow pit
And help him balance at the edge.

I clean him with fresh leaves
And crumpled fast food napkins from my coat pocket.
The soiled paper flutters in my hands like prayer flags.
The old man smiles at me and whispers,
"Daughter, there is much honor in shit work."

Alabama Bound

Margaret Rozga

Names whispered to history, now nearly lost:
McNair, Collins, Welsey, Robertson.
Jackson, Reeb, Daniels, Liuzzo.
Some of the rest of us still alive.

We follow a map fitting words to terrain
much as personal history intertwines
with snatches of headlines and refrains of songs,
Oh, Wallace, you never can jail us all,
much the way the land becomes place, home, the past.

Here's the map awake with history:
Montgomery, Anniston, Birmingham, Montgomery,
Selma, Dallas County, and again Montgomery
through Lowndes County and back. Bus boycotts.
Interstate buses. Bull, his dogs, hoses. Deaths and more deaths.

A cross-weave against that warp:
the Edmund Pettus Bridge across the Alabama
River out of Selma. *Oh, Wallace,*
though cotton kings still loom across the landscape
Segregation's bound to fall.

Summer 1965. Days down dirt roads,
days of chopping and picking, registering,
days begun before sun up and ended with mass
meetings in tin-roofed churches, never mind the rain,
never mind the unnatural threats. Vote hope.

Now new years. Rain stops. Churches rebuild
red brick, and tin is sent for recycling.
Museums open, and historical markers go up.
Polls seem to speak for voters. I hope yet for better,
for more. Birmingham and Montgomery begin to look
unbound, try hard to stay out of the news.

Eulogy for Prathia Hall Wynn

"Faithful Love and Loyalty join together,
Saving Justice and Peace embrace." Psalm 85:10 (JB)

Wilda Morris

Night riders whose shots
grazed your skin could not deter you.
The deputy whose bullets danced
around your feet, who threw you
in a Georgia jail, could not defeat you.
State troopers and their horses
on Bloody Sunday on Edmund Pettus Bridge
could not destroy you or your dream
of that elusive embrace of justice and peace
toward which you edged.

Even when you saw the wicked
swallow the righteous, the poor
sold for a pair of sandals, their heads
trampled in the dust, and glory
stolen from the children of your people,
even when faith trembled, still you believed.
Like Moses, you peered into that land
of promise not yet fulfilled.

Was that enough?

Peace March

Dane Cervine

Scottish bagpipes were the reason,
the belly dancers rhythmical pulse,
or maybe it was the flags:
American, United Nations, Earth,
Bahai youth handing out heart stickers
emblazoned with *there is no room here for hatred.*

It could have been
the Spanish dancers, children in blue, red, white dresses
clicking hard-toed heels to music that says
every country is mine, with no lines to cross
but the curve of horizon glinting dark then light,
the satellite eye true—blue & brown, water & ground
all that lies beneath.

Armies are blind, but not the ones who point them,
   this is the reason
children were marching, this is the reason
Arab congregation, Jewish temple, Christian lesbians,
politicians for peace turned out
For this day

the art of survival, a new revival,
each shoe looking for another
to walk in

before the other shoe drops.

AGING

Belinda Subraman

Three daily pigeons on a rock wall,
each in different stanch,
each stiff-still
in a listening pose...
to a dog barking,
a child's cry in a house nearby,
an ice cream truck
with its primitive, repetitive lullaby.

We hear motors on the road,
a plane in the air,
wind-finger chimes from tinkles to forest rain,
the flow of a pool, a water fall,
a creek or an ocean.

Even with children screaming
We are dreaming ...
homilies, hopping birds, plants.
We are retiring or unplugging
from the shallow anxiety of living,
not quitting
but becoming involved with our souls
if not buried in distraction electronically
or side tracked sexually.

It's an anywhere summer day
when it dawns on us
that time just adds wrinkles,
we supply the meaning.
These are our lives
passing by.

NO MORE AIDS

Paul K. Pattengale, MD

No more AIDS
    with the speed dating craze?

No more AIDS
    in a metrosexual daze?

No more AIDS
    with anti-virals out of phase?

No more AIDS
    when Jesus saves?

No more AIDS
    when Africa fades?

No more AIDS
    when the big boys have paid?

No more AIDS
    when mortals behave?

No more AIDS
    in the enlightened New Age?

No more AIDS
    when the planet is razed,

No more AIDS
    when we're all in our graves,

No more AIDS
    when *the* vaccine is made.

Out of Line

Our Lady of Sorrows
Mauren Tolman Flannery

In the procession, *Viernes Santo*,
she rises above their heads
like balloon bunches
propagating in the plaza
in front of the crowded church.
She is *La Dolorosa*,
the sorrowful mother,
and she wears the permanent
expression of an urban beggar.
Seven daggers pierce the heart
exposed on her breast
like a silver cactus leaf.

    The first sword of sorrow
    was forged of Simeon's prophetic words
    spoken in the temple to the mother of the child
      And thy own soul
      a sword shall pierce.
    It was the thought of their
    innocent babies' future pain.

The queen of melancholy
rides in her somber palanquin
as her subjects begin to follow her
through cobblestone streets.

    An angel thrust the second
    with her warning to the husband
    against something like the death squads of the state.
      Take the child and His mother,
      and flee into Egypt: Herod will
      seek the child to destroy Him.

They know about this journeying,
this being strangers in a strange land.
In unison they sing their sorrows,
chant their disappointments,
breathing her incense breath
as it floats upward, taking their
losses with hers into the night sky.

   The third was the sorrow
   that she kept inside her heart
   the strange lonely sorrow
   of each twelve-year-old's own mother.

She journeyed with her child to the temple,
lost Him in the columns
among the thoughts and thinkers,
took a stimulated stranger home again.
Come all who pass by the way.
Look and see how there is still suffering
so like unto my suffering.
Weep for yourselves
and for your children.

Past their own homes
they follow her elevated grieving,
these women who worship her wounded heart:
the mothers of the disappeared;
the one whose man went North
and was not heard from,
the one who visits a tiny grave
defined with plastic roses
now bleached in the sun
to a sick creamy pink;
the woman whose daughter
married away and has isolated herself

with her bruises and her babies;
the mother, pregnant again,
whose prolapsed uterus spurns its task
as curious children question
her about the blood.
She is the *curandera* who carries
on her head the suffering of women
like a bundle of laundry

> The fourth stiletto was the face
> of her boy as He faced His executioners.
> The fifth fell upon her
> with the falling of His blood,
> and the sixth was the weight of His
> lifeless body in her weak, weary arms.
> And the seventh was His grave.

She is the widow, the spinster,
the mother of fighters, the abandoned, the barren,
the bearer of more than she can feed.
Her deep blue mantle cloaks their griefs
and their wails are for her Son and their own.
Devoutly they follow her seven sorrows exposed,
raised up, and moving like a slow thick fog
through familiar streets where they live them.

What to Say About Jake
Sarah Werthan Buttenwieser

Last spring, my nearly three-year-old son, Lucien, went through a weeklong "boys only" phase, during which he was constantly asking, "Is __ a boy or a girl?" (Girl was pronounced in the guttural, "guul.") One evening, as I tucked him into bed, he announced that he only liked one of his teachers, Jake—"for Jake's a boy, and I like boys."

So I asked what makes a boy a boy and a girl a girl. "Boys are boys because of resolution," he informed me. My mind flashed to Jake, and it occurred to me that Lucien was right. I was somewhat stunned by Lucien's insight. But, in signature three-year-old fashion, he continued, "Girls are girls because of caddy." Lucien—like the rest of us—had no idea how to answer my question.

For us parents, Jake's story began the previous November. Parents received two letters, the first from the school's early education coordinator, the other from Hope, one of the four teachers in the Toddler Room. Both letters informed us that Hope would soon make a gender change, a long considered decision on her part. The school had contacted experts to offer advice about how best to facilitate this experience for our children. After Christmas break, the kids would refer to Hope by his new name, Jake, and the identifying pronoun would switch from she to he. Teachers and administrators expected that over the first weeks, parents, teachers and children would slip up on the name and the pronouns. Parents were assured that such mistakes were fine. The hormones, which Hope had already begun to take, would cause gradual changes in appearance. No science fiction transformation was imminent. Still, over the coming months, Jake might develop more body and facial hair, his voice might deepen and his body's shape might be altered. However, the person the kids knew and loved would still exist, and the kids would feel loved as before, just by Jake rather than by Hope. The school arranged an evening meeting with a psychologist for parents to ask any questions they might have.

Most of us first met Hope when she began teaching our toddlers late in the summer. A rather androgynous looking, small woman with cropped dark hair, Hope favored baggy pants, a button down shirt over her T-shirt and clunky work boots. My first impression of her, glimpsing her from across the playground on a hot August morning, was that she resembled a fifteen year-old-boy. One parent later told me about an older child, who, when he was in Toddler Room, told his parents, "Well, Hope is a boy," when describing his teachers. Other people said that from afar, they hadn't been sure whether Hope was a she or a he. In the small, progressive, lesbian-friendly town of Northampton, Massachusetts, Hope seemingly fit in, as work boot wearing, jean clad, shorthaired women are practically ubiquitous.

My heart was beating a little faster by the time I finished reading these letters. Hope's news surprised me, particularly since I'd never been close to anyone who had made this choice. To suffer enough that she would deem such a drastic choice necessary was, to me, unfathomable. At the same time, I felt privileged to come into contact with such a momentous experience in another person's life. It seemed like a special responsibility to be supportive of her (him?) throughout this period of transition, even transformation. During our years as parents at the daycare center, we'd supported teachers through other life-changing events: having babies, being diagnosed with diabetes, losing worldly goods to a house fire... This teacher-related development was certainly interesting. Thinking about Hope, I returned again and again to her size: she was a small woman who would be a tiny man. Most of the other parents seemed to share similar combinations of protectiveness and supportiveness, perhaps a somewhat skeptical, almost guarded sort of enthusiasm.

I did not worry for a moment about the response from or well being of my two-and-a-half-year-old son, Lucien. He, like all the kids in the classroom, adored the quietly magnetic Hope. They would love Jake–the same person, after all–just as much. Besides, gender seemed meaningless to Lucien and his peers at that time.

His fellow toddlers were all just about the same age as he was: the oldest kids would turn three over the winter; the bulk of these kids had spring and summer birthdays; the youngest child would turn three September first.

At the parents' meeting, a nervous, practically giddy air filled the room. People had questions: how quickly would he look different? How much detail did we need to go into with our toddlers and how much detail did we need to go into with our older children? How did the other teachers feel? One person asked whether the synthetic male hormones would cause him to be violent. Another asked whether seeing this woman change her gender would cause her own child to want to change his gender. Not surprisingly, little was yet known about how children respond to adults' gender changes, except for when their own parents are the ones to make those transitions, a situation very different from ours in school. We learned that the physical changes tend to be gradual and that the hormones did not induce violent behavior or urges. The few parents voicing their fear of children's exposure to the situation reminded me of the homophobia that had reportedly surfaced in many school communities when gay and lesbian teachers first came out in those environments. What seemed shocking to us in 2000 might be relatively–in our progressive community–commonplace years down the road. Two (out the ten teachers present) who balanced on the low, child-size chairs in the room that evening were lesbians.

That first morning after the holiday break, I felt nervous as I pulled the classroom door open. "Hi, Jake," I said. His new name did not roll easily off my tongue. That was Hope, wasn't it? It was like addressing an actor in character; although he looked the same (he looked like Hope), he had a new name, a changed identity. And I liked Hope's name, besides. Markers, set upright into a board, were ready on one table; a pretend fire truck and many fire hats occupied the dramatic play area. At a dawdling pace, I filled out the sheet where parents noted how long our children had slept and what they'd had for breakfast. I noted that in the classroom, there were a total (never all in the class at once) of three girls and thirteen boys. Then, I confessed to Jake and the other teacher present that

I'd said nothing to my child about Hope's name change until we were in the car driving over that morning. "I didn't know exactly what to say. I didn't want to inflate this for Lucien." As it turned out, the kids had practiced calling Hope by both names throughout December.

Over the summer, six months after the transition, I set out to discover what had transpired for Lucien's classmates at that time by talking to their parents.

Some parents had discussed the upcoming name change with their kids over the Christmas break. Eamon's parents spoke with their son the day of or the day before school vacation ended. "Hope's changing his name to Jake."

"No!" Eamon exclaimed. A moment later, he asked, "Who will be Hope?"

His mother answered, "I don't know."

Eamon offered, "Daddy will be Hope." Eamon stuck with "Hope" and "Hopie" for perhaps a month to six weeks, then switched to Jake.

Brandon, who called Hope, "Hopie," almost like a nickname, did not want to call him Jake right away. His mother noticed that once Brandon accomplished a shift in pronoun use–he rather than she–the proper name, Jake, followed. The pronoun switch from female to male was a little difficult for Duncan, who used he and she, her and him interchangeably, anyway, as did many of his peers. Soon after the name change, when Duncan's parents asked who was at school that day, if they asked, "Was Jake there?" Duncan responded, "Hope." They'd point out that Hope's name was now Jake. He simply agreed, "Right." For a long time, Zachary used the name, "Hope/Jake." Most parents corrected their kids when they referred to Jake as "Hope." Johnny continued to call Jake, "Hope," even through the following summer and his mother never corrected him.

Indeed, during those snowy winter weeks early in January, parents and children switched names and pronouns: Hope, Jake, him, her, she, he. And that was fine with the teachers, including

Jake. Over the course of the spring, Jake did experience gradual physical changes. His voice dropped somewhat lower; more body hair appeared; his upper body bulked up considerably. Without fanfare, Jake had surgery to have his breasts removed. Other than the fact that he couldn't lift the kids during his recovery, nobody even seemed aware of this physical change.

Initially, some of the kids had ideas about these two people, Hope and Jake. Brandon wondered, "Does Jake have two birthdays now? One for Hope, and one for Jake?" Julian once suggested to his mother, because of Jake's new name: "We could have a birthday party for her." Emmett, who had just turned three at the time, seemed not to notice any change. One afternoon, though, he proposed changing his own name. "Jake can do it, why can't I?" And Zachary explained, "Jake's a boy. Hope's a girl."

The kids didn't exhibit awareness of a significant change. Miriam, for example, was not curious about Hope's name change. Her father doubts whether she remembers that Jake had ever been Hope. Eamon's mother said, "I suspected this transition would be easy for the kids, which might have helped. Maybe if they'd been four or five it might have been harder, but I think kids are very flexible." Olivia's father echoed this observation, noting that Olivia's awareness of any change was "fairly minimal." Her older brother was four at the time. He was aware of the transition and asked a few questions as to why and how, yet was non-judgmental of the change and of the premise that someone could make that choice. This parent admired his children's reactions, musing, "If only we could all be that open to changes and transitions..."

Some of the parents believed that their children might have had difficulty if another of the teachers, other than Hope, had made a gender change. Ryan's mother thought he might have had a harder time if Kelly or Jen had made a gender transition, since Ryan was much more aware of their gender than of "Hope/Jake's." If the physical changes had been more dramatic, she believed Ryan might have displayed a stronger reaction. Similarly, a mother with twins, Alex and Ella, thought that if Cathy, her kids' favorite teacher, had made a gender change, her daughter especially would have been distressed. Ella spent a lot of time in Cathy's lap and might have been confused by Cathy's making this kind of change.

For the most part, what transpired during the rest of the academic year was that the two-year-olds turned three. Their language burst from short sentences to longer ones. Their ability to pretend blossomed. The puzzles had more pieces; the stories had more words and pages. The songs got longer. Their climbing got higher. In the classroom, Jake, Kelly, Cathy, Lori, and Susan supported their astonishing growth.

Certainly, it's hard to imagine a time when such transitions would be commonplace. During the winter and spring of 2001, a group of fifteen families with toddlers learned that to have a teacher execute a gender change can be relatively easily weathered. Our collective goodwill–Jake's for entrusting us; the parents' for being supportive; the kids' for being themselves–was rewarded, because the transition went smoothly. Certainly, in a progressive community, with the implicit backing of a college administration that had no choice except not to discriminate due to gender bias, an infrastructure supported this experience. A high school teacher might be someone parents meet once or twice a year. The relationship between parents of toddlers and their teachers is intimate. We were invested in our kids' teachers because we knew how important they were to our children. The happier he would be–Jake, Hope, whoever–the better for our children.

What parents reported was that they thought the transition loomed larger for them than for their children. One parent reported that she remains "somewhat confused by someone's desire to do something so drastic," and finds herself wondering sometimes what this transition is like for Jake. "Who does he feel like?" For some, the hardest part was simply getting used to a new set of pronouns. One parent described the situation as easy "because this is such a liberal community, and because all of the adults already knew and adored Hope, and thus wanted the best for her. Parents wanted to be supportive."

Other parents agreed with both of her points: the desire to be supportive, and certainty that the social climate–milieu, as one parent put it–would help with the transition. Another parent described how this community's progressive makeup, coupled with the fact that parents were accepting of these changes, meant that the situation was normalized. In another social environment, she imagines the same situation would cause a much larger stir. When she received the letters in November, another parent's reaction was "only in Northampton. This could only happen at the Campus School. Wow. The letter left Hope so exposed, it was so public." Reading the letter, she was struck by how miserable Hope must have been, and hoped that as Jake, he'd be happier. She found Hope to be so even and stable that she was surprised by the depths of Hope's unhappiness. Initially, though, she did have a concern about whether the drugs would have any effect upon Jake's personality. She thought that no visible change was apparent. Another parent felt the experience was much more traumatic for her and her husband than it was for their son. She believed the school mishandled the situation. The school's administration, in her opinion, should not have gone into so much detail. Her own worries centered upon how the transition would affect the kids and whether the kids would be safe. Describing the meeting between parents and mental health experts, she noted, "Those therapists were talking about families, and Jake is not my family." Instead, she thought that the school's administration had an opportunity to downplay this experience, but that Smith College–and the town of Northampton, even–encouraged it to be too big a deal.

Most of the parents, though, expressed appreciation for the way the school handled the situation, and thought the right amount of attention had been paid.

In retrospect, much of what probably shook us all up was that Hope's decision to alter this most–in our minds inherent–determinant challenged the notion that gender is a fixed entity. As Lucien noted, she/he had added resolution to the equation. No longer could we say to our children, definitively, that gender was what it was just because it was. After knowing Hope/Jake, if a child of ours were to want to switch genders, we could no longer respond that this was impossible. We would have to hold that possibility open. We might dissuade our child, seek therapy on his or her behalf, attempt a host of other measures before truly contemplating this radical option, but it exists for us, and therefore, for our children. The difference between the mother who expressed this fear during the parents' meeting and what I'd characterize as reality is this: Jake can't, by mere example, force a child to want to change gender (nor would he want to do so). However, for a child, who inherently might find gender change a healing choice, knowing Jake could be important: like seeing a door you assumed to be sealed shut miraculously pushed open. One of the preschool teachers said as much, "There are children I've taught, just one or two, who I can imagine were not born into the gender they would feel happiest being. For these kids, knowing someone like Jake would be very important."

Having a relationship with Jake changed certain of our assumptions. His experience alters the way we envision the world and the way we explain the world to our children. It's not unlike the changes wrought by the presence of an increasingly visible and family oriented gay and lesbian population. Whereas, once it might have been sufficient to envision a typical family as mother, father, child or children, this has now changed significantly in many of our communities. There might be two moms, after all, or two dads. As we confront new realities, our language, and our sense of expectation, shifts. What we learned by knowing Hope and Jake forced us to see gender as malleable rather than rigid. Perhaps, our kids will eventually come up with satisfactory answers for what makes a boy a boy and a girl a girl. Or maybe, for them, this won't even matter.

Praise

Aida K. Press

Praise the sunset
glorifying the darkening sky
Find me a doe alert
not moving
in the glen

Show me pond lilies
bursting into bloom
rain dimpling
an errant stream

Discover a blood red
cardinal singing
against a royal sky
Pavarotti
in a maple tree

Savor the tomatoes
ripening in your garden
enough eggplant and zucchini
for our whole neighborhood

This is the gift
you give to me, my love:
the ecstasy of simple things.

Eve

Aida K. Press

She wasn't prepared
For the Rage of God
In the waterless desert
The dry cruel wind
Lacerating her weed-clad body
No shade trees
No fruit waiting to be picked
No guardian angels
Adam ceaselessly berating her
I told you not to
I told you not to
So cold at night
So hot in the sun
And yet, she didn't regret
That bite of the apple
That sweet taste
Of knowing.

The House in Roskilde
For Else and Henning

Donna Pucciani

This is the house of blue rooms,
cool walls the color of sky and sea.

A yellow photo album
enfolds spirals of memory:
a white-haired matriarch, one beloved
sister who hanged herself in a cellar,
another the sunny-haired girl whose voices
drove her from a fourth-story window,
two smiling daughters now grown,
and a holiday flat huddled on a hill
in the south of France.

The house is warm, holds heat
and hope. On the table, three white candles
on silver stems twined with buds
and green ribbons bless the cerulean damask
set with honey, butter, cheese, and tea poured
from a pot the color of soil and twilight.

This is the house of blue rugs,
dusty blue in the parlor,
oriental peacock in the dining room
spread-eagled on brown floorboards,
gray-blue carpet creeping up the stairs.

In winter the lady of the house,
dreading the long Scandinavian nights,
takes morphine for pain, reads books
in three languages, watches the sky darken
thickly, shattering into shards of snow.

Her husband the schoolmaster,
eyes like gray doves,
takes his tea and toast in bed
then cycles to school to fight
for the union and teach recalcitrant
students the vagaries of English grammar.

In summer she bikes down the lane,
glossy hair flying in the wind off the fiords
that float ahead in fronds of mist.
Spinning down the cobbled coast road
she passes the village church and the fisheries,
buys a bag of apples at the market
under skies of white-hot noon.

Their lives mesh the way canals
web the city in nets of water and light,
the terrors of November wind lingering
into February trances that melt finally
in the evening sun of June, summer's
ubiquitous optimism holding them captive
in the nightlong cooing of doves
woven by the beak of the blackbird
nesting in the ivy, whistling past midnight.

A Learned Response

Barry Ballard

    The man I just passed turned away, as if
making eye-contact would have threatened
his anonymity (a learned response
learning how to master the body it
inhabits). So there was nothing but a wish
that we had transcended the cold system
we created, that we could have (just once)
stepped outside those shadows that exist

in a separate world completely detached
from their own buildings. There was nothing to step
ahead of us and break up the path,
forcing us to pause and recapture
our humanity, nothing to correct
our image-glaring in the monuments of glass.

The Garden

Barry Ballard

Sometimes when downtown in the neon glare,
you can see things glowing in your body
that sunlight fails to detect, a layer
of someone else reaching (almost timidly)
for the blood-red roses on every street
corner. It's always the place where you turn
when memory is fed, when the mind competes
for beauty where the hanging street lights burn.

And you know the air should be sweet with voices full
of the fragrance of civility, that the hands
soiled and reaching from the sidewalks should end
in bright blossom, elegance, and armfuls
of symmetry, and that the dying should stand
as if the sun was saying,"Let's start again."

CONTRIBUTORS

Diana Anhalt's essays and poetry have appeared in, among others, *Grand Tour, Jewish Currents, The Comstock Review, Passager* and in various anthologies. Author of *A Gathering of Fugitives: American Political Expatriates in Mexico 1947-1965*, she is a book reviewer for *The Texas Observer*.

Barry Ballard's poetry has recently appeared in *The Evansville Review, Blue Mesa,* and the *Florida Review,* among others. Recent collections are *First Probe to Antarctica* (Bright Hill Press Award) and *Plowing to the End of The Road* (Finishing Line Press Award and nominated for Pushcart Prize).

Jonathan Barrett lives in Kansas City with his wife, Megan, and two sons, Elijah and Gavin. He works in Ameriquest Mortgage Co. His recent work has appeared in *North American Review, William and Mary Review,* and *Wisconsin Review,* among others.

Kristin Berkey-Abbot teaches English and Creative Writing at the Art Institute of Ft. Lauderdale. She has published in many journals and has a chapbook, *Whistling Past the Graveyard* (Pudding House Press). She has work forthcoming in *Poetry East* and *South Carolina Review.*

Carol Pearce Bjorlie is adjunct professor of music at the University of Wisconsin, River Falls, and poetry/creative process teacher at the Loft Literary Center in Minneapolis. Her poems appear in *Southern Poetry Review, Great River Review, St. Andrew's Review,* among others.

Alice Bolstridge has publications of fiction, poetry, and creative nonfiction in a wide variety of literary magazines and anthologies, including *Maine Voices* (Milkweed, forthcoming), *Nimrod, Cimarron Review,* and *Passager* (1995 Passager Poet Award).

John Bradley is the editor of two anthologies: *Atomic Ghost: Poets Respond to the Nuclear Age* and *Learning to Glow: A Nuclear Reader.* Curbstone Press will soon publish his poems, *Terrestrial Music.* He teaches writing at Northern Illinois University.

Sarah Werthan Buttenwieser, a longtime reproductive rights and community activist, spends most of her time raising three boys and writing fiction and nonfiction. Her work has appeared in *Hip Mama, Moxie, Jewish Currents,* and *The Georgia Review,* among others.

Douglas G. Campbell's poetry has been printed in a number of publications, including *Riversedge, Rockhurst Review,* and *Ann Arbor Review.* He teaches art for George Fox University and has exhibited his artworks in over 130 exhibits throughout the U.S.

Sharon Carter obtained her medical degree from Cambridge University and now works in a health center in Kitsap County. Her poems have appeared in *Raven Chronicles, Heliotrop,* and *Synapse,* among others. Co-editor of *Literary Salt,* she received a Jack Straw Writers award in 2003.

Susan H. Case is a college professor in New York City. Recent work can be found in *Ariel, Asphodel, Floating Holiday, Freshwater, Mad Poets Review, Slant, Stray Dog,* among others. Her chapbook, *The Scottish Cafe',* is being translated into Ukrainian.

Michael Casey's first book *Obscenities* was in the *Yale Younger Poet Series,* edited by Stanley Kunitz. His later books are *Millrat* (Adastra Press, 1999) and *The Million Dollar Hole* (Orchises Press, 2001). His latest book is *Raiding a Whorehouse* (Adastra Press, 2004).

Dane Cervine lives in Santa Cruz, California, where he serves as Chief of Children's Mental Health for the county. His work has recently appeared in *Eclipse, Freshwater,* and *Raven Chronicles,* among others. He has also published in several recent anthologies.

Brent Christianson lives in Madison, Wisconsin, where he is Lutheran Campus Pastor and Director of the Lutheran Campus Center of the University of Wisconsin-Madison. He has been published in *Off the Coast, Out of Line, The Wisconsin Poets' Calendar,* among others.

Alice D'Alessio worked as publications editor at the UW-Madison. She has published articles, poems, and *Uncommon Sense: the Biography of Marshall Erdman.* She was runner-up in the Wisconsin Academy of Arts, Letters, and Sciences poetry contest.

Florence Chard Dacey has published two collections of poems, *The Swoon* and *The Necklace.* A recipient of a Loft McKnight Poetry Award, she was the featured writer in *Great River Review.* Her work has appeared in numerous journals and anthologies.

Adam D. Fisher is Rabbi Emeritus of Temple Isaiah, Stony Brook, NY. He has published eight books, including two books of poems, *Rooms, Airy Rooms* and *Dancing Alone,* as well as *An Everlasting Name on the Holocaust and God's Garden,* short stories for children.

Maureen Tolman Flannery's newly- released *Ancestors in the Landscape: Poems of a Rancher's Daughter* has been nominated for a Pulitzer Prize. *A Fine Line* was also published this year. Her other books are *Secret of the Rising Up: Poems of Mexico; Remembered Into Life;* and the anthology *Knowing Stones: Poems of Exotic Places.*

Courtney Lea Franklin lives in San Diego, where she is working on an MFA in Poetry at San Diego State University. She is an activist, teacher, and poet. She also tutors young writers and works as an Assistant Editor for *Poetry International.*

Anthony Garavente is a university lecturer in history at California State University, Dominguez Hills, and UCLA. He has nineteen stories accepted for publication, and has two unpublished novels and a novella: *Baseball, Birthright,* and *Curse of the Cat: A Faded Photograph.*

Joseph Gastiger, pastor at the First Congregational United Church of Christ in Dekalb, Illinois, has published in *TriQuarterly, Poetry, College English, Out of Line, Luminous Stone,* among others. He has long been active in antiwar and social justice work.

Michael H Gavin is a professor of literature at Prince George's Community College where he is advisor for the literary magazine. He has publications forthcoming in *Oyez Review, The Oak, Basics of Speech, Poetry Motel,* and *Curbside Review,* among others.

Jacqueline Guidry's novel, *The Year the Colored Sisters Came to Town,* received the Thorpe Menn Award for literary excellence, was chosen as the 2003 United We Read book for Kansas City, and was selected for the Pen/Faulkner Writers in Schools program.

Barbara Hoffman is a high school English teacher. Her poetry has appeared in *Minnesota Review, Beloit Poetry Journal, Blue Mesa Review,* and other journals. She received a Fellowship to Virginia Center for the Creative Arts, Sweetbriar, Virginia.

Bette Lynch Husted's works include a collection of inter-related memoir essays about relationship to land and its consequences, *Above the Clearwater: Learning to Live on Stolen Land* (Oregon State Univ. Press) and a poetry chapbook, *After Fire* (Pudding House, 2002).

Joan Payne Kincaid, nominated for Pushcart Prizes in 1998 and 1999, has two books out in 2004: *The Umbrella Poems—drawings and poems with Wayne Hogan,* and *Snap Shoots, A Collection of Oriental Forms of Poetry.* She lives in Sea Cliff, Long Island.

Susanna Lang has original poems, essays, and translations from the French in *Kalliope, World Literature Today, Chicago Review,* among others. Her translations include *Words in Stone* and *The Origin of Language,* by Yves Bonnefoy. She teaches school in Chicago where she lives with her husband and son.

Steven Larson has published in small magazines and did a chapbook with may apple press, *Fishing the Wide River.* He is a public school teacher, musician, and grower of organic peppers.

Sean Lause has published criticism in *The Winesburg Eagle,* fiction in *The Mid-American Review,* and poetry in *Poetry International, Poetry Motel, Bathtub Gin,* and *European Judaism,* among others. He teaches English at Rhodes State College in Lima, Ohio.

Richard Levine's manuscript, *What Light Will Bring,* was a finalist for the Ohio State University Press Poetry Book Award, 2003. *Snapshots from a Battle,* a chapbook, was published by Headwaters Press. His poems appear in *Comstock Review, North American Review,* and *Thema,* among others.

Sara Littlecrow-Russell is a family law attorney whose award-winning political poetry, articles, and research have appeared in a wide variety of magazines, journals, and anthologies including *The Indigenous Women's Health Book: Within the Sacred Circle* and *Sister Nations: Native American Women Writing on Community.*

Lyn Lifshin has published more than 100 books of poetry; her poems have appeared in most literary and poetry magazines, including *Out of Line*; and she is the subject of an award winning documentary film. Her recent books from Black Sparrow Press include *Before It's Light* (Paterson poetry award) and *Another Woman Who Looks Like Me.*

Maura Madigan lives in Dubai, United Arab Emirates, with her husband and daughters. Her fiction, non-fiction, and poetry has appeared in *The Summerset Review, The Arabia Review, Blueline, Women's International Network Magazine, Escape from America,* among others.

John McBride lives in Bettendorf, Iowa, with his wife, Nancy. Before retiring, he was a university teacher, administrator, and social worker. He has won numerous poetry awards, and his work has appeared in *The Christian Science Monitor, Poetry Motel, and Common Threads,* among others.

Mario Milosevic's poems have appeared in many journals, including *Black Warrior Review, Rattle, Light Quarterly,* and *Nerve Cowboy,* and in the anthology *Poets Against the War.* He works in a small town library in the Pacific Northwest.

Prudence Todd Moffett ended up a social worker after a long spell as a minister's wife in inner city parishes. Now she is a writer. She has appeared previously in *Out of Line* and has published recently in *Pikeville Review* and *Journal of Kentucky Studies.*

Patricia Monaghan is the daughter of a Purple Heart veteran of the Korean War and a member of the Society of Friends. Author of three books of poetry, most recently *Dancing with Chaos* (Salmon Poetry), she teaches science and literature at DePaul University in Chicago.

Bob Monson was a Czech linguist in the Army (1959-62), taught high school English in Oregon for 35 years, retired, and began writing for publication. He has a poem in *Verse Weavers* (Oregon State Poetry Assoc.) and a story in *Clackamas Literary Review.*

Billie Morrill is a Reference Librarian at the East Lyme Public Library in Niantic, Connecticut. Her poems have appeared in various journals, including *Skylark, The Underwood Review, The Lullwater Review,* and *Mature Years.*

Wilda Morris is the coordinator of Shalom Education, an ecumenical organization providing curriculum and workshops on peace and justice issues. She is editor of *The Pebble* and the author of *Stop the Violence! Educating Ourselves to Protect Our Youth.*

Steven Morr-Wineman is a mental health worker, writer, parent, activist for nonviolent social change, and survivor of childhood trauma. He is the author of *Power-Under: Trauma and Nonviolent Social Change* (www.TraumaAndNonviolence.com).

Richard Newman is a poet and essayist whose work has appeared in *The American Voice, On the Issues, Prairie Schooner,* and *Birmingham Poetry Review,* among others. He is Associate Professor in the English Department of Nassau Community College.

Adnan Adam Onart is a Bostonian poet of Crimean Tatar descent, born and raised in Istanbul. In addition to his Turkish poems, his work in English appeared in *The Boston Poet, Prairie Schooner, The Massachusetts Review, Red Wheel Barrow,* and others.

Paul K. Pattengale MD is Professor of Pathology and Microbiology at the University of Southern California Keck School of Medicine and is a practicing pathologist at Childrens Hospital, Los Angeles. He has recently completed a medical thriller entitled *The Master Cure* and is working on a collection of short stories.

Joel B. Peckham, Jr.'s poems and essays have been published or are forthcoming in many journals, including *The Black Warrior Review, The Dalhousie Review, Nimrod,* and *Prairie Schooner.* His poetry book, *nightwalking,* was published by Pecan Grove Press.

Shirley Powers is the author of *With No Slow Dance* (Two Steps In Press, Palo Alto, CA). Her work has also appeared in *Earth's Daughters, Iris, Iowa Woman, Wisconsin Review, Out of Line*, among others. She won First Place 1995 Encore Poetry Magazine Contest.

Aida K. Press is editor emerita of the *Radcliffe Quarterly*. She has studied with poets Ruth Whitman and Kinereth Gensler and is currently a student of Susanne Berger. Her poems have been published in *Out of Line* and in the anthology, *Women Runners, Stories of Transformation*.

Donna Pucciani, Vice-President of the Poets' Club of Chicago, has published reviews, articles, and poetry in *Maryland Poetry Review, Wisconsin Review, Mid-American Poetry Review*, among others. She has won awards from the Illinois and Florida State Poetry Societies and Poets & Patrons of Chicago.

David Radavich's recent poetry collections are *By the Way* (Buttonwood, 1998) and *Greatest Hits* (Pudding House, 2000). His plays have been performed across the U.S. and in Europe. He currently is working on a scholarly study of Midwestern drama.

Gemette R. Reid moved away from academic writing, where she had won publishing prizes, to poetry. She read "Snow Drops" by invitation to the Boston Research Association in Cambridge. She has published poetry in *Harvard Alumni Journal* and others.

Joseph Ross lives in Washington, D.C. His writing has appeared in several literary journals and magazines such as *Sojourners, The Other Side,* and *The Washington Post*. He has also been published in *D.C. Poets Against the War: Anthology*.

Deborah Rothschild lives in Houston, Texas, and writes essays, short fiction, monologues, and poetry. She has raised three daughters, been married three times, and has lived on three continents. Her work has been published both in the U.S. and abroad.

Margaret Rozga publishes poetry, short fiction, and creative non-fiction narratives. Her work has appeared in literary journals, including the *Porcupine*, the *Kerf*, and the *Chaffin Journal*. Rozga is a professor of English at the University of Wisconsin-Waukesha.

Joanne Seltzer, of Schenectady, N.Y., has poems in many journals and anthologies, including *The Village Voice, The Minnesota Review, When I Am An Old Woman I Shall Wear Purple*. She has also published fiction, essays, translations of French poetry, and three poetry chapbooks.

Marian Kaplun Shapiro lives in Lexington, Massachusetts, where she practices as a psychologist and poet. Her poetry–three of her poems have won awards–has appeared in literary magazines. She has published *Second Childhood* (Norton, 1989) and many journal articles.

Melissa Shook is a retired professor in the Art Department at the University of Massachusetts at Boston. She has a national exhibition record in photography and is a recipient of a National Endowment Award in the Visual Arts. She writes non-fiction and poetry.

Adam J. Sorkin's translations have been published widely. Recent volumes include *The Bridge* (Bloodaxe Books, U.K.), Marin Sorescu's last book, and three books in 2003: *Diary of a Clone* by Saviana StÂnescu, *Singular Destinies: Contemporary Poets of Bessarabia*, and *41* by Ioana Ieronim(Bucharest).

Judith Sornberger is a professor in English and Women's Studies at Mansfield University of Pennsylvania. Her work has appeared in distinguished journals, chapbooks, and anthologies. Her book of poems, *Open Heart,* was published by Calyx Books in 1993.

Belinda Subraman's poetry, stories, and art can be found in over 400 journals, reviews, anthologies, and chapbooks. Her archives have been housed at the University of New Mexico, Albuquerque. Belinda is a Registered Nurse specializing in hospice care.

Christina Trout, a New Mexico native, student, wife, and mother, now lives in Northern Colorado. An accomplished artist, artisan, gardener, cook, Christina now finds her voice in prose and poetry.

Lidia Vianu, poet, novelist, critic, translator, and Fulbright lecturer, is a professor of English at the University of Bucharest. Vianu's recent book of literary criticism is *British Desperadoes at the Turn of the Millennium.* She has published three poetry collections in addition to her five books of translations.

Tom Whalen's poetry and fiction have appeared in *The Georgia Review, The Idaho Review, The Iowa Review, Chelsea, Northwest Review,* and other journals. *Winter Coat,* a poetry collection, appeared with Red Dust in 1998. He lives in Stuttgart, Germany.

Judy Wilson teaches Creative Writing at Southwest Minnesota State University. She has appeared in many literary journals, including *Mississippi Review, Antietam Review,* and *Caprice.* She has received awards for fiction, including the Truman Capote Fellowship.

Bryan Thao Worra is one of the first Laotian American Poets. His work has appeared in *Unarmed, Whistling Shade, Journal of the Asian American Renaissance,* and the anthology, *Bamboo Among the Oaks,* among others. He lives in Minnesota.

Kristin Camitta Zimet is the editor of *The Sow's Ear Poetry Review*. Her first collection of poems, *Take in My Arms the Dark*, appeared in 1999, and her second is nearing completion. She works as a nature guide in the Shenandoah Valley.

Fredrick Zydek has published five collections of poetry. *Ending The Fast*, his third, included a quartet titled *"Songs from the Quinault Valley"* which was awarded the Sarah Foley O'Loughlen Award. His work has appeared in *The Antioch Review, Poetry, Prairie Schooner,* and others.